Sherlock Holmes

The Treasure of the Poison King

By

Paul D Gilbert

Paperback 978-1-78705-786-9
ePub ISBN 978-1-78705-787-6
PDF ISBN 978-1-78705-788-3

MX Publishing
335 Princess Park Manor, Royal Drive,
London, N11 3GX
www.mxpublishing.com

Cover design by Brian Belanger
www.belangerbooks.com and www.redbubble.com/people/zhahadun

Author of:

The Lost Files of Sherlock Holmes

The Chronicles of Sherlock Holmes

Sherlock Holmes and the Giant Rat of Sumatra

The Annals of Sherlock Holmes

Sherlock Holmes and the Unholy Trinity

Sherlock Holmes: The Four Handed Game

The Illumination of Sherlock Holmes

Contents

Introduction

Upon the completion of my trilogy, with The Illumination of Sherlock Holmes, I was consumed, not only by a sense of great satisfaction, but also by a wave of exhaustion.

So much so, in fact, that I even toyed with the idea of a long hiatus perhaps followed by a return to the short story format. However, upon being introduced to the charismatic and oft ignored character of Mithradates VI, the King of Pontus in the first century BC, I immediately threw myself into a frenzy of research with a desire to introduce him, both to Sherlock Holmes as well as to my readers.

I sincerely hope that you will share my enthusiasm and excitement for this endeavour. As ever, my long-suffering wife Jackie deserves both your consideration and sympathy, together with my eternal gratitude!

PDG

Chapter One: The King of Pontus

When, in 63 BCE, Mithradates VI of Pontus; also known as Mithradates Eupator Dionysius or "The Great" and "King of Kings," died at his own hand, he had reached the astonishing age of 72 years.

Of course, this would have been a remarkable and grand old age for any man living in those times, but for a prince and then king who had lived and flirted with death throughout the entirety of his long and turbulent life; this had been even more miraculous!

The young Mithradates had been brought up within the royal household of the ancient kingdom of Pontus at a time when plotting and assassinations had become almost commonplace within those great halls of power. His own mother, Laodicea had seized control of the kingdom by poisoning her husband, Mithradates V, and upon realising that Laodicea had started to show greater favour towards Chrestus, his younger and more malleable brother, the teenage Mithradates decided to remove himself from harm's way.

The young prince decided to sacrifice the trappings and temptations of his capital and the luxuries of the palace and he slunk away unnoticed, under the cover of night. In exchange, he now voluntarily suffered the hardships and dangers of wandering throughout the remotest and harshest wildernesses of his kingdom.

The years that the young Mithradates spent in voluntary exile would stand him in good stead once he returned to claim his birth right. In order to just to survive, Mithradates soon became highly skilled in the arts of hunting and endurance, and during the course of his harsh education; he had come close to death on more than one occasion.

During this time, Mithradates began to accumulate a vast knowledge of the ways of poisons. He had been fortunate enough to have cheated death after having digested a bunch of berries, which appeared to have looked harmless enough at first glance, but had in fact possessed a deadly toxin within their juicy interiors. Mithradates realised that knowledge of such toxins would prove invaluable to him within the treacherous halls of his palace and the fate of his father immediately came to mind.

Legend claims that he had ingested such vast amounts of various toxins, during his sojourn in the wilderness that by the time of his unexpected return he had made himself immune to any that might have been used against him. Indeed, the universal antidote that he had created became much sought after in his own times and even up to the present day. Mithradates had been determined that he should not suffer the outcome of so many of his close relations and he returned to court confident in his true worth and power.

His very presence and determination belied his relative youth, for he was still in his late teens and his immediate action, was to have both his mother and younger brother arrested and thrown into the dungeons! Neither of them would survive their incarceration, and within a very short period of time Mithradates' right to rule and   reign over Pontus had been both universally recognised and confirmed.

With every obstruction to his rule now removed, Mithradates steadily grew in confidence and ambition and he lost no time at all in expanding the Pontic kingdom. In order to consolidate his inherent aura, the young king proclaimed himself to be a descendent of both King Darius of Persia and Alexander the Great. Although history has failed neither to confirm nor deny this illustrious lineage, his subjects lost no time in accepting his grandiose claims and word soon spread amongst the neighbouring kingdoms, that the days of Alexander's glory had returned.

Remarkably, although everyone has heard of Hannibal and Spartacus, two of ancient Rome's deadliest and most threatening of enemies; the name of Mithradates has somehow escaped the same level of historical scrutiny. Nevertheless, the threat that he and his armies posed to the survival of the Roman Republic and its imperial ambitions, had been every bit as real and threatening,

His first foray beyond his own borders had come at the behest of the various Hellenistic settlements of the Crimea who had sought his protection from their many enemies. This assistance Mithradates had been only too happy to provide them with, but it had come at a great cost; namely the independence of these kingdoms!

He then formed a tenuous alliance with a relative of his, King Nicomedes III of Bithynia. Their combined forces soon annexed both Paphlagonia and Colchis, but even these developments had failed to ignite any real interest from those venerated members of the Roman Senate.

Furthermore, even Mithradates' annexation of Colchis in 103 BC, failed to galvanise Rome into action. This had been partly due to the vast distance that separated the two centres of power, but also the fact that Rome had been actively involved in other theatres of war at that time. Indeed, it was not until 94 BC that Rome finally acknowledged the threat that Mithradates had posed to it and thus its relentless military juggernaut began its progress towards the East. So began the first Mithradatic war.

This conflict did not begin well for the Romans. Mithradates, through both diplomatic and military means, had made great progress in Cappadocia and even Greece itself, and it was not until sufficient funds had been raised that Lucius Cornelius Sulla Felix, a Consul, general and would-be dictator, had been able to strike out for the threatened provinces of Asia Minor.

However, it was at this point that Mithradates made a serious tactical error. In a misguided attempt at consolidating and unifying his newly won territories through fear and terror, he ordered the slaughter of more than 80,000 Roman and Italian citizens who had been living peacefully within those provinces. This ruthless and some would say, self-destructive action, had the unfortunate effect of intensifying Sulla's determination to strike against the King of Pontus, and before long the Roman Consul was engaging the armies of both Mithradates and his allies throughout the entire blood-soaked region.

In the year, 85 BC, having suffered a heavy defeat at the battle of Chaeronea, Mithradates finally sued for peace. The awful realisation, that even his superiority at sea had been diminished by the fleets of the Roman general Lucullus, compelled him to agree to an unfavourable treaty. The truce that then followed, however, had been only a brief and tenuous one and two years later, once Sulla had returned to Rome, his general Murena disobeyed his orders and launched an invasion of Pontus itself, under his own volition.

This time it was the Romans who were forced to taste the bitterness of defeat. Murena's campaign had lasted for less than a year, and after the cataclysmic battle of the river Halys, the errant general had been forced to sue for peace and he then had to endure an ignominious return to Rome. It had been at this time that Mithradates had bestowed upon himself the rather grandiose titles of "King of Kings" and "The Great," and the people of his lands rejoiced at his success.

As a result of the civil wars that had raged between the armies of the dictators Marius and Sulla and their draining effects upon both finances and resources, it would be another eight years before Rome was able to return its attention towards Mithradates and its lost provinces in Asia Minor.

Under the command of Lucullus, a general who Sulla knew was worthy of his trust, an outnumbered Roman army won decisive victories, firstly in Pontus itself and then finally in Armenia, where Mithradates had enlisted the help of his son-in-law, King Tigranes. By now the depleted forces of the beleaguered king were in full retreat and Lucullus knew that a decisive victory was assured.

However, the naive general was robbed of the final taste of triumph when the politicians back in Rome decided to recall him in favour of another member of the Triumvirate, the more influential and venerated Pompey the Great. Pompey pursued Mithradates to the last of his territories, the lands that lay to the north of the Black Sea.

To add to his woes, Mithradates also had to contend with the rebellion of his own treacherous and cowardly son, who saw the plight of his father as the perfect opportunity for him to seize his undeserved power prematurely. By now, even the ever-buoyant King knew that all hope was lost and thus the King of Pontus decided to take his own life.

According to the historian Cassius Dio, the magnificent and tragic irony of Mithradates' attempted suicide had been the effectiveness of his own 'universal antidote!' Repeated attempts at self-poisoning had ended in abject failure, and as the forces of Pompey drew ever closer, the Poison King finally acknowledged the efficacy of his antidote in despair. As a last resort Mithradates entrusted his servants with the sorry and unenviable task of ending their king's life. Amidst much wailing and lamenting, they armed themselves with spears and swords and slew each of Mithradates' daughters and wives before ending their ruler's life with as much dignity as they could. At least Mithradates had been spared the ignominy of being led through the streets of Rome as part of Pompey's triumphal return.

Historically, the Mithradatic wars had the effect of hastening the demise of the Roman Republic, a violent process that finally led to the ascendancy of Imperial Rome. Following the collapse of the Triumvirate, a succession of costly and bloody civil wars soon followed. The last of these, culminated in the death of Marc Anthony and Cleopatra and the appointment of Rome's first Emperor, Augustus. As a consequence, Mithradates will always be assured of his place in Roman history, although not in the manner that he might have imagined or relished. Notwithstanding this, it had been Pompey the Great who had enjoyed the trappings and glory of a Roman triumph.

The return to Rome of Lucullus had been somewhat less auspicious than that of his great rival, although he had been able to console himself with the thought of the contents of his treasure ships, the booty that he had plundered from the Necropolis of Amisos just prior to his summons back to Rome. Despite the loss of one of those ships to a violent storm, close to the coast of Greece, Lucullus had at least assured himself of a most luxurious retirement with the contents of those ships fortunate enough to have survived the tempest.

Only myths and legends have made reference to the contents of that sunken Triconter[1]. Some of these tales have alluded to sea chests overflowing with precious jewels and vessels fashioned from pure gold! Others have made mention of the remarkable Antikythera Mechanism[2], an intricate calculating device that had boasted dozens of intermeshed gears and more cogwheels than the most

---

[1] *A large Roman merchant ship*

[2] *A legendary early form of computer*

advanced of modern time pieces! This ancient computer had been capable of performing the most complex of calculations, and it was even said that it could track the movements of the planets, the constellations and the distant galaxies that lay beyond.

There had even been rumours of an engraved tablet aboard, upon which had been inscribed Mithradates' legendary "universal antidote", to some perhaps, the most desirable of all of those treasures.

Nevertheless, these great prizes had long been condemned to the depths of those treacherous seas and lost forever to the realms of myth and legend. That remained the case throughout the millennia, until the year 1901 AD when a small group of Greek sponge divers made a remarkable discovery............

****

Chapter Two: The Three Pledges

After months of agonising and fear of the inevitable, it had been towards the end of October 1901 that my dear wife, Sophie, had finally received the news that she had been dreading throughout that time. After a long illness, her beloved Aunt Lydia, the same lady who had provided Sophie with shelter and sanctuary at a time when her life had been under threat, had finally passed away peacefully, within her small- holding near Frinton on the coast of Essex. Obviously my wife had been greatly upset by the loss of her only aunt and understandably she had decided to attend the funeral.

It was agreed that she would travel down to Frinton with her brother, Simon Sinclair, and due to the small and intimate nature of this family gathering, I was to remain in London while they finalised Aunt Lydia's affairs. It would be the first time that we had been separated since our marriage, three years previously and due to my medical practice's tawdry situation, I soon found myself at a loose end in her absence. Inevitably, my thoughts turned at once towards my old lodgings at 221b Baker Street and my very good friend, Mr. Sherlock Holmes.

The year 1901 had, thus far, yielded very little in the way of cases challenging enough to satisfy my friend's not inconsiderable skills and abilities. Indeed, apart from the matter at the Priory School[3] and the disappearance of

---

[3] By A.C.D.

Lady Frances Carfax[4], I can think of no other occasion when I had been invited to collaborate with him upon one of his adventures.

Optimistically, I packed my overnight bag and hailed a cab for Baker Street. The greeting that I had received from my former landlady, Mrs. Hudson, had been everything that I could have hoped for. However, the same could not have been said of Holmes' lacklustre welcome. His dishevelled appearance told of an extended period of inactivity and his pallid complexion and reddened eyes indicated to me the inevitable personal abuse that Holmes had often subjected himself to as a result of his being unemployed.

He waved me towards my old chair with an apathetic arm and grunted a form of incomprehensible greeting through a sardonic smile.

"So Watson, I see that Mrs. Watson's favourite aunt has finally departed this mortal coil and as a result, the prodigal son has returned." Holmes pronounced, while inviting me to help myself to tobacco from his Persian slipper.

I took him up on this offering without a moment's hesitation, for I could already tell that Holmes had fallen into one of his darker, more acerbic moods.

"You should not look so surprised Watson, for I remember you telling me of Aunt Lydia's illness during your last visit and the presence of your bag merely confirms her fatality."

---

[4] By A.C.D.

"I understand, but perhaps my imposition has come at a bad time for you" I suggested through a plume of blue, pungent smoke.

My tone had clearly roused Holmes from his aura of self-pity and he rose suddenly to go to his room.

"There is no such thing as a bad time for a visit from my old friend. I shall be with you once I have attended to my toilet." There was now a positive jaunt to his step as he left the room and when he reappeared shortly afterward, he was as well-groomed as I had always remembered him.

It almost felt like old times when Mrs. Hudson appeared unannounced bearing a substantial lunch tray and Holmes observed my surprise when he joined me in its voracious consumption.

"As you have no doubt observed it has not only been my grooming that has been neglected of late, and I am certain that my dereliction would not have met with my doctor's approval had he been present," he said mischievously.

"Very likely not!" I said in a scolding tone. "However, do I not observe a slight tremor of excitement that speaks of the imminent end to your malaise?" I stated speculatively.

"Hah! Oh Watson! Your skills of deduction have certainly not diminished with time. I trust you will stay to take notes?" Holmes asked as he pressed a calling card into my eager hand.

"Of course I will! I can assure you that there is more than just a toothbrush and night shirt in my bag."

The card, although of the very finest quality, was somewhat scant of information. It merely stated the intention of Lady Roberta Wakeham of Holland Park, who wished to call upon 221b at precisely 1 p.m. that very afternoon.

"Why Holmes, that means that we have barely a few moments in which to complete our lunch." I exclaimed with not a little dismay in my voice.

"You are quite right Watson." Holmes agreed, but to my consternation, he immediately called down to Mrs. Hudson and requested that she remove our lunch things without a moment's delay.

Mrs. Hudson had clearly been as aggrieved as I at such neglect, and she grumbled to herself as she left the room bearing the tantalising tray. It did not take me long to find my notebook and pen, and Holmes and I even had the time to fill our pipes before we heard the ring of the bell pull that announced the arrival of our new client.

By the time of Lady Wakeham's arrival, the weather outside had taken a considerable turn for the worse. A typically violent October storm had taken hold and Baker Street was being bombarded by a torrent of grey, chilly rain and a veritable tempest of howling winds. The trees that lined Baker Street had been twisted and contorted into grotesque caricatures of their usual stately selves and the gales had shrieked through every crack and crevice.

We had been assured of the gravity of Lady Wakeham's situation by virtue of the fierceness of the conditions that she must have endured in reaching us in the first place. She had clearly dispensed with the convenience and shelter of a carriage, for her hooded cape was soaked through and her hair, once it had been finally revealed, was bedraggled and in dire need of a thick warm towel.

Holmes was on to his feet in an instant and he draped the lady's outer garment over the back of a chair close to our fire before showing her to a seat adjacent to his own. An instant later Mrs. Hudson arrived bearing a tray of steaming coffee and some feminine care and comfort. We allowed our weary visitor a moment or two of warm indulgence, before gently inquiring as to the nature of her predicament.

Lady Roberta Wakeham was a slim statuesque woman in her early sixties with whom time had dealt most kindly. It had not been hard to visualise her as being very attractive in her youth, and she had lost neither her poise nor posture with the passing of the years. She spoke with a light, modulated tone and her smile was a soft and gentle one. She sat uneasily on the edge of her chair and she seemed to be reluctant to reveal the reason for her visit.

"You have endured much in your efforts at reaching my door on such a day, and I observe that your right hand still shakes, despite it having been warmed by the fire and Mrs. Hudson's coffee. Pray, explain to me how I might be able to aid you at this trying time. Remember that you should exclude nothing, no matter how trivial it might appear to be and you can be rest assured that the discretion of my colleague, Dr Watson, may be relied upon as surely as that of my own." Holmes was leaning forward, with his elbows resting upon his knees; however his tone was invitingly modulated as opposed to his usual authoritative pitch.

"You are very kind, Mr. Holmes, although I do hesitate in setting this matter before you, such is the somewhat outré nature of my distress."

"Lady Wakeham, you should have no concerns on that score, for Mr. Holmes positively recoils at the very notion of the commonplace." I smiled as I readied my notebook and pencil.

"Well said Watson. Please begin Lady Wakeham." Holmes sat back into his chair, clasped his hands together and closed his eyes in a deep, meditative state of concentration.

"You should know at the outset, Mr. Holmes that my late husband and I fell in love and were married at a very early age and that we had remained as such throughout our forty years together, right up to the moment of his untimely death last Halloween. That is not to say that we enjoyed forty years of continuous, unbridled bliss. Of course, that is not only impossible, but I am not even sure if such a status quo is desirable.

"My husband, Henry, had inherited both his considerable fortune and his vast estate and therefore had neither the need nor the inclination to do a day's work throughout his entire life. Naturally, he had received a most excellent education, but he used this to hone his undoubted talent as a poet, a passion which he had enjoyed since his early childhood. His great gift and boundless energy having been rewarded with the publication of many of his collections, and he has even enjoyed a form of celebrity as a result of this."

"Ah of course, I am very familiar with his work!" I exclaimed, much to my friend's obvious annoyance. Lady Wakeham gently tilted her head in appreciation before continuing.

"Mr. Holmes, you should know that my late husband had his demons, as is quite often the case amongst those great romantic poets, amongst whom my husband can certainly be numbered.

"On those, not uncommon, occasions when the words refused to reveal themselves to him and his inspiration had failed to motivate him, he was prone to drown his angst and frustrations in a frenzied orgy of drinking. He was never abusive or violent during these Bacchanalias, you understand, but he did take himself off to the far wing of the house, where he felt that he would cease to be the cause of any distress to me. In that he was correct and successful, however, during the course of these excesses he was also liable to abscond to a small, exclusive gentlemen's club, whose name escapes me, where he would quite often gamble away a considerable sum of money!" Lady Roberta was clearly distressed by these horrendous recollections, quite understandably I should say, and she stopped to delicately blow her nose and draw a deep breath or two, before quietly apologising for her protracted pause.

"Although I had not realised this at the time, Henry had almost drained the coffers dry, although I would have been powerless at preventing him even if I had known of this. He had always been most discreet in all of his indulgences and all matters of business and finance had remained within his exclusive domain. It was only several months after his passing that his creditors began arriving at my door."

"Calm yourself, Lady Wakeham, for you are surely amongst friends here," I offered. She smiled gratefully and continued.

"My ignorance regarding our affairs, prompted me to seek the advice of one of our oldest friends and Henry's solicitor of many years standing, Sir Cecil Blanding. It was only now that the full horror of my situation revealed itself. Blanding searched through each and every one of Henry's books and papers and finally came to the deplorable conclusion that my only hope of staying out of the courts and avoiding public ruin, was to sell up the estate and pay off Henry's debts with the proceeds of the sale! Naturally such a concept was abhorrent to me."

Despite the stoic comportment of so many of her creed, this last revelation proved to be too much for Her Ladyship, and Holmes waved me impatiently towards her, that I might calm and comfort her. Meanwhile, Holmes had leapt up from his chair and hurriedly lit a cigarette by the window.

"Lady Wakeham, as distressing and unfortunate as your predicament surely is, I fail to see how any crime has been committed, save for your late husband's reckless disregard for your future well-being. I am afraid that my humble practice has no means of paying off his debts for you," Holmes pointed out with an unnecessarily acidic air.

Lady Wakeham suddenly stood up and raised herself to her full, not inconsiderable height.

"Mr. Holmes, I shall disregard your discourteous manner, in the hope that notwithstanding your tone, you might yet prove to be of some use to me. I shall tell you something now that I hope you will regard with a totally open mind, rather than that of the pragmatic sceptic that I would normally have expected.

"You see, I am well acquainted with Dr. Watson's accounts of some of your adventures and I am aware that you regard matters of the heart with a derisory distain."

"I cannot deny it," Holmes admitted apologetically, and he suggested that Her Ladyship return to her chair with a wave of his hand.

"Henry and I were unashamedly romantic, Mr. Holmes and had been from the moment that we first met all those years ago. That is why I know that he would never have left me in this predicament without having first made provision for such an eventuality. He made three pledges to me, Mr. Holmes, the nature of which might seem absurd to a man of logic like you, but they meant everything to me."

"Three pledges?" Holmes repeated impatiently and Lady Wakeham nodded her head defiantly and emphatically.

"In his darker moments, Henry's thoughts and quite often his work turned to the nature of death and its aftermath. He believed that should we two remain in love and faithful to the other, it would transcend even death itself. I have remained true to this pledge and despite all that has befallen, my love for him has kept him alive, in my heart at least, or so I thought."

"Lady Wakeham, please!" Holmes was clearly becoming exasperated by Her Ladyship's most extraordinary declarations.

To her credit, she ignored Holmes' ire and persisted with her explanation.

"Henry further pledged that should anything happen to him, he would ensure that adequate provision would be made for every eventuality that might befall me. Obviously Cecil Blanding's revelations caused me to believe that Henry had sadly failed me in that at least, but I had not allowed for the unlikely results of our third pledge."

Holmes' impatience and irritation had, by now, transformed into a marked indifference. Consequently it was I who inquired further into Her Ladyship's true meaning.

"What exactly did you mean when you said 'or so I thought' when referring to your enduring love?"

"I used that phrase, Dr. Watson, because I now have good reason to believe that Henry has not really left me at all! Before you admonish me further, for your refusal to accept a supernatural explanation is well known to me, Mr. Homes, I must tell you that I am not a young girl prone to flights of fancy. I have good reason for my doubts. I shall quickly explain my meaning before you dismiss me." Holmes eyed her quizzically with knitted brows.

"Henry and I first became acquainted at a recital held at the home of a mutual friend of ours, in Holland Park. Our eyes met as they began to play a passage of music that we subsequently discovered to be our favourite piece: *Danse Macabre* by the French composer, Camille Saint-Saens. From that moment the music became forever embodied within the soul of our romance, so much so in fact that Henry wrote a poetic accompaniment to the piece.

"I loved the poem as surely as I did the music itself and subsequently we both pledged that it should remain within our private domain for all of time. Indeed, we further vowed that it should remain so, even after death and that the survivor would place the poem within the coffin of the other, sealed forever from public gaze. The dire consequences of his compulsions had left poor Henry a broken man and his health suffered and deteriorated beyond repair. Mercifully, his end had been brief and without pain. With his final breath he thrust the poem into my trembling hand.

"I kept my promise, Mr. Holmes and the poem of 'Danse Macabre' has resided within my husband's coffin from the day of his passing, a year ago today."

"Madam, you have yet to explain why you hold the belief that your husband has somehow managed to defy man's ultimate destiny," Holmes stated simply, although now clearly intrigued by our client's tale.

24

"Not surprisingly, my belief is beyond your realm of understanding, Mr. Holmes, nevertheless I would appreciate your logical explanation for the fact that this envelope came through my letter box this very morning!" Her voice rose to a trembling crescendo before she sat back breathlessly.

Lady Wakeham offered Holmes a plain, unmarked buff envelope, but he directed it in my direction. Somewhat hesitantly I pulled out two folded sheets of foolscap; however, they nearly fell from my grasp when I saw the heading at the top of the first sheet.

"Danse Macabre." I read in a hushed deferent tone.

At once Holmes returned to his seat and pursed his lips with his left forefinger.

"Read it Dr. Watson, please read." Lady Wakeham implored and Holmes nodded his acquiescence.

On an unholy night such as this,
Two lovers glow in eternal bliss
And so they dance

Turning to each other they exchange a kiss
And swear to the other a lovers' Trist,
And still they dance

The night of the spirits closes in,
And soon their wailing creates a dreadful din,

25

They will dance for evermore, evermore.

So still the night, starry bright night

The flying clouds betray a lustrous moon,
The lovers start to sway and swoon,
And still they dance.

They are drawn towards the unearthly sky,
And feel as if they can truly fly
As they dance.

The music of the spirits calls to their soul,
But still they meld and closer hold
And still they dance.

The demons sing and the night grows cold
Lovers shuddering not so bold
Their swirling slows as the cockerel crows,
Their spirit fades.

Their skin turns white as the spirits fall; they fade to
naught as the gravestones call
The dawn is king and they dance no more, no more....
Nevermore

It seemed an age before another word was uttered and it fell to me to break the silence.

"What a truly remarkable and evocative piece of work."

Holmes dismissed my remark with an impatient wave of his hand. He reached out hungrily for the envelope, surprisingly ignoring the sheets of poetry that had been folded within, and then began to examine it meticulously with his smallest glass.

"Lady Wakeham, as you so correctly observed I have no truck with ghosts and the like, so I will ask you to dispassionately explain to me how this envelope happened to come into your possession. There are no letters or markings upon it, so it had obviously been delivered by hand before you awoke, by someone wearing a meticulously clean pair of gloves. The stationary is of the very finest quality and bears a water mark that is unique in my experience."

"I have no theory, Mr. Holmes, other than the one that I have already presented to you. I believe that my husband has never truly left me, just as he had pledged. However, I must tell you that the word 'nevermore' did not appear upon the version of 'Danse Macabre' that had been buried with him! Nevertheless it is impossible that anyone else had ever seen the original, much less embellish it with a single, superfluous word!" By now, Lady Wakeham had worked herself up into a frenzy of utter confusion and she glared imploringly towards my friend for help.

I too looked to Holmes for any sign of sympathy or compassion. After all, he had surely been presented with a case that under normal circumstances he would unhesitatingly dismiss out of hand. Yet, when the distracted lady had mentioned 'nevermore' my friend's countenance had suddenly altered, and he had disappeared into one of his protracted, contemplative dispositions.

Holmes turned away from us both and as he lit his pipe he murmured: "Please leave your address and that of your solicitor with Dr. Watson. We shall be with you within the hour."

Clearly Lady Wakeham had not taken kindly to being so dismissed, but she allowed me to hold the door open for her with good grace and paused long enough to ask me for an explanation. My enigmatic friend had left me no wiser than Her Ladyship, and I merely answered her entreaties with a woeful shrug.

Anticipating my pent-up barrage of questions, Holmes turned towards me with a winning smile.

"Watson, we must not allow ourselves to be beguiled by Her Ladyship's wild tales of eternal love and poems of the supernatural. If we are to be of any use to her at all we have to examine her conundrum with calm and dispassionate logic. I am certain that you would concur with the probability that Lord Henry Wakeham did not resurrect himself and leave his coffin merely to add one word to the end of a poem, even to one as special as 'Danse Macabre'?"

"Well of course I would! However, she does hold her beliefs with such heartfelt conviction, that it would be a travesty to break that spell before we have discovered another resolution. Why would her husband have left her in such a financial dilemma, especially after having made so sincere a pledge?" I asked.

"I take it that you have never heard of C. Auguste Dupin?" Holmes' surprising response had been such a departure from the nature of our discussion that I became totally nonplussed and incapable of a coherent reply.

Holmes continued as if my answer, had there been one, would have been a total irrelevance.

"Dupin has been my portal into the world of Edgar Alan Poe. Although an acquired read, Poe has achieved a form of notoriety for his tales and poems that test the nerves of those brave enough to delve into the darker realms. Poe also introduced the world to the notion of an amateur consulting detective, namely C. Auguste Dupin, who featured in his tale 'The Murders in the Rue Morgue.'"

"I confess that I have not read his work, but now I certainly understand your interest in the man." I admitted.

"Judging by Lady Wakeham's reaction to the word 'nevermore,' I would wager that she has never sampled Poe's work either. Now, however, I suggest that we hasten to Farringdon!"

"You must mean Holland Park, surely?" I queried, but my friend was already dressed for the harsh elements beyond our door and half way down the stairs, by the time I had realised that no reply was to be forthcoming.

We had stepped outside into an unrelenting sheet of the variety of fine and insidious rain that seems to permeate every pore and sinew. Yet my friend seemed to be singularly unaffected by and indifferent to this meteorological inconvenience and once we had hurriedly boarded a cab, he sat perched on the edge of his seat, while leaning upon his tightly furled umbrella.

Holmes had been as good as his word and upon reaching a small but discreet address in Farringdon, he alighted from our cab and dashed off without even an indication of his purpose. He returned, a few short minutes later, flushed with excitement and success, while holding aloft a blank sheet of paper as if in a moment of great triumph.

"I think that we can safely say that we now know the source of Lady Wakeham's resurrected poem!" He beamed.

"No doubt you hold a sample of Cecil Blanding's stationary and that it bears the same water mark as does the poem?"

"Oh Watson, you absolutely radiate insightfulness today!" My friend declared with a jovial sarcasm.

"I suppose that Lord Wakeham had entrusted a copy of his poem into the care of his solicitor, with the instruction that it should only be delivered to his wife at a time of crisis. However, apart from its otherworldly significance to Lady Wakeham, I fail to see how we are any closer to delivering the poor woman from her awful plight." I declared quietly, but my friend remained in a thoughtful silence until the moment of our arrival at the Wakehams' address in Holland Park.

A long, beech-lined driveway soon revealed a spectacular white marble mansion, whose grand entrance was flanked by a magnificent set of Ionian pillars. On other nights one could easily have imagined each of the large undraped windows illuminated by a festoon of crystal chandeliers while the sound of gaiety and music filled the air outside.

Tonight, however, each of the many rooms were shrouded in a melancholy darkness, save for one and our wheels churning through the ever-enlarging puddles was the only recognisable sound. A grave sadness seemed to have been hanging over the entire edifice and a cheerless butler met us at the door.

Tyler, this faithful servant, tried to present us with a smile of greeting, yet even his sparkling, bespectacled eyes could not disguise the gloom of the household. On our way to the drawing room, where Her Ladyship pensively awaited us, Tyler offered us a warming glass of cognac which we eagerly accepted.

Despite the blaze of a large roaring fire, there had been no escaping a surprising and voracious chill that seemed to fill the entire room. We soon discovered its source when a violent gust of wind blew the drapes into a wild billow and a cascade of rain and leaves sprayed onto the floor in front of us. Lady Wakeham scolded her servant harshly for his oversight, although he had assured her that he had left the window securely locked when last in the room.

Ignoring this disruption, Holmes readily accepted a seat by the fire and he smoked a cigarette while he sipped his brandy. Suddenly he turned towards our hostess.

"Lady Wakeham, I can tell that you did not share your husband's enthusiasm for the works of Edgar Allan Poe," he stated simply and without explanation.

"Although true, that is a somewhat unusual assertion for you to have made. Mr. Holmes." Her Ladyship had been clearly put out by my friend's statement, as if she had been expecting something more illuminating from her reluctant ally. Then she noticed something in my friend's manner that suggested to her that there had been an unforeseen significance to his claim.

"Mr. Holmes, throughout our marriage I had always made a point of trying to appreciate and share in my husband's passions, save of course for those destructive indulgences that he reserved for his club. In most instances this had not been something that I had found hard to do. Our tastes in music and literature seemed to run along similar paths anyway and we obtained great pleasure and satisfaction in each other's company, regardless of the chosen activity.

In the case of Edgar Allan Poe, however, I did find it difficult to understand my husband's enthusiasm. Undeniably I tried to appreciate Poe's work; indeed at times I would lock myself away with one of his stories, in the hope that an epiphany would eventually come upon me. Sadly this did not happen, I found his style unbearably dark and morbid, if not disturbingly psychotic at times, but I was at least successful in constructing a convincing facade that my husband would never breach. However, I do fail to see how you came to that conclusion."

"That does explain his use of the word 'Nevermore'" Holmes said self-indulgently under his breath. "Madam, would you be so kind as to show me through to the library?" Holmes requested whilst rising hurriedly from his chair.

Lady Wakeham appeared to have been as taken off guard and confused, by this request as I had been. Nevertheless, she immediately pulled upon a bell rope and a moment later Tyler appeared, bearing a bright oil lamp before him. We climbed slowly to the first floor and all the while Tyler's flame flickered and occasionally ebbed as the gathering storm outside forced its' way through the tiniest fissures, thereby creating a series of grotesque shadows that seemed to dance upon the walls.

The library proved to be a large, elegant room, laid out in the spacious, Romanesque style of the Georgian era. On Holmes' demand, Tyler turned up the gas and Holmes immediately began a frantic, but thorough search through the section predominated by books of poetry. Not surprisingly it did not take my friend long in finding a selection devoted to the works of Poe, but he seemed to concentrate upon those volumes more particularly devoted to "The Raven."

Again, I could not offer Her Ladyship a single word of explanation for my friend's unfathomable behaviour and this took a further turn when he began to flip the pages of each book back and forth in the most fierce and urgent manner imaginable. Finally, with a pronounced grunt of disappointment, Holmes sank slowly to the floor upon his haunches, as if bereft of energy and ideas.

We three exchanged glances of bewilderment, while my friend continued to crouch there, in a breathless silence. Then something else occurred to him and he rose slowly with a languid elegance and something akin to a suppressed smile upon his inscrutable face.

"Lady Wakeham, did your husband keep a smaller, more personal library, wherein he might have also done his writing?" Holmes asked expectantly.

"Indeed he did, Mr. Holmes, although I cannot for the life of me understand your obsession with the books of Edgar Allan Poe." She was clearly becoming exasperated by my friend's inexplicable conduct, whereas I knew from experience that there was a logical purpose behind each one of his actions.

"Very likely not, however it is your husband's devotion to the works of Mr. Poe that holds the key to your salvation. Did he by any chance refer to this room as his chamber?"

Lady Wakeham's open-mouthed incredulousness proved to be the only confirmation that Holmes had required.

"Tyler, kindly show me to the chamber and would you also be good enough to bring with you a ladder?"

"A ladder sir?" The butler asked, but without another word Holmes fled from the room, bounded up the stairs and began a speculative exploration of the darkened corridors of the floor above.

By the time that Tyler had arrived with his light and ladder, Holmes had already found the object of his search. He had been staring up at the arch above a small solid doorway and the statues that adorned the columns on either side of the arch. On the left I could recognise a marble bust of the Titan Pallas, while on the other rested a rather fearsome, jet black raven.

The wind outside howled raucously as we gazed up at this formidable bird and the flickering flames of Tyler's lamp seemed to imbue a fiery, spectral light to the creature's eyes. Holmes bade the butler to focus the flames upon the plinth beneath the raven's claws and we all drew gasps of wonder when we recognised the words that had been engraved into its' base......... "Nevermore"!

In a thrice Holmes had extended the ladder and an instant later he found himself face to face with the raven's menacing beak. Despite my entreaties that he should take care, Holmes wrapped his arms about the creature and began to grapple with the cement that bound it to the plinth. Despite almost losing his balance on more than one occasion, Holmes eventually prised the raven loose, and he handed it carefully down to me before making his descent.

"It is deceptively heavy Holmes." I stated simply, while my friend could barely suppress a triumphal smile.

He led us back down the stairs to the drawing room and placed the raven in the middle of the table before sending Tyler for the "sharpest knife in the house." As we waited for the tireless butler once again, Holmes lit a cigarette and gazed at his mournful prize.

In anticipation of a myriad of questions from both Her Ladyship and me, Holmes began his explanation through a plume of slowly exhaled smoke.

"Lady Wakeham, I fear that had you not sought my consultation, your own, though well-intentioned, deceit would have rendered your husband's subtle clue as worthless."

"My deceit, Mr. Holmes, whatever can you mean?"

Holmes diverted his gaze from the bird to Her Ladyship.

"Your pretence for a love of Poe led your husband to believe that you would understand in a trice his addition of the word 'Nevermore' to his poem. For that is the name of the raven in his most famous work. 'Perched upon a bust of Pallas above my chamber door,' I believe is an approximate quote and one that Lord Wakeham would have expected you to recognise at once. By the way, that envelope had not been delivered from beyond the grave, but from the offices of Blanding and Blanding of Farringdon," Holmes' concluded.

"As usual Holmes, your reasoning is quite flawless, but I still fail to see how the statue of a bird will prove to be her Ladyship's salvation." I said, no doubt echoing the thoughts of our bemused client.

At that moment Tyler returned with a most sturdy and fearsome looking instrument that Holmes snatched from his grasp without hesitation. He raised it to the raven's left wing and gently scratched away a slither of thin black paint.

"Good heavens Holmes, it is only paint! What does this all mean?"

"It means Watson that despite Lord Wakeham's other flaws and weaknesses, he did keep his final pledge. Unless I am very much mistaken, this imposing bird is made of nothing less than solid gold, and Lady Wakeham's future has therefore been secured!" Holmes pronounced while grabbing his hat and gloves from the astounded butler.

By now, Lady Wakeham who had hitherto remained enwrapped in a stunned silence, sank into a chair and held out her hand that Tyler might fill it with a glass of cognac.

"How will I ever thank you, Mr. Holmes?" She asked with a breathless smile before taking a sip of her drink.

Holmes dismissed this with a smile and a wave of his hand.

"Lady Wakeham, your gratitude should rather be directed towards your husband and of course, to Mr. Edgar Allan Poe! Come Watson!" I followed in my friend's wake and a moment later we were sheltering from the equinoctial storm, in our cab.

As we reached a bend in the driveway I had been afforded a brief glimpse of the brightly lit drawing room, wherein I had imagined Lady Wakeham, still seated in a state of elated exhaustion. However, she had since moved to the window and I could see her endlessly and rhythmically twirling in time, no doubt, to the imagined strains of *Danse Macabre*.

Had it been my flight of fancy, or perhaps the distorted movements of the bare twisted branches of the beech? Or was someone there with her, locked in a timeless embrace, '*while they danced*'?

****

Chapter Three: The Rabbi

The sense of unease that I had felt, even a long while after we had left the home of Lady Wakeham, had soon been dispelled by Holmes' suggestion that we should celebrate the satisfactory conclusion of the case with a late supper at Simpson's of Piccadilly. It had been a suggestion with which I had wholeheartedly concurred, especially once I had realised that we had just enough time to secure a table before they closed.

Despite this most joyous celebration of a gratifying case, by the time that we had finally arrived back at Baker Street my thoughts had turned again to the fact I had yet to receive word from my beloved Sophie as to her proposed date of return from Frinton. I must admit that I became poor company for the remainder of the evening and my subsequent night's sleep had been both restless and fitful.

After a hurried breakfast the following morning, I found myself on the way home, long before Holmes had even roused himself from his bed. Doubtless, my disappointment upon finding nothing more than a small pile of bills upon my door mat might be well understood. I spent but a few moments in ensuring that the house had been secure and that everything else had been in order, before embarking upon a slow and disconsolate journey back to my friend.

I had only been absent for a short while, yet during my brief time away Holmes had not only dressed and breakfasted, but I had also found him to be engaged in an earnest conversation with an old associate of ours, namely, Menachem Goldman. I had not been exactly overjoyed at the sight of Goldman sitting there, for I had never really approved of his profession, nor the fact that Holmes had sought his help and advice on more than one occasion.

However, it was also true to say that had it not been for Goldman's expertise and advice, we should not have been able to locate the missing Venetian mandolin, nor the whereabouts of Baron Gruner and his mysterious Bavarian castle, at the conclusion of our search for the third member of the "Unholy Trinity."[5]

Despite any misgivings that I might have harboured, I had to admit that Menachem Goldman was one of the most anomalous individuals that I had yet encountered. To aid his discreet movements within the more insalubrious regions of the jewellery market, he had adopted the impenetrable disguise of an orthodox Polish Rabbi and I would defy even a fellow adherent of his faith to deny that he was indeed a Jewish man of learning. Goldman's accent had always been flawless and he liberally sprinkled his conversations with phrases in Yiddish.

Although not a language in itself, this hybrid of German, Russian, Polish and Hebrew, was so expressive and possessed so many appropriate sounding phrases, that it had been slowly finding its' way on to the streets of the East End of London. Even I had picked up a smattering of the easier to pronounce expressions!

---

[5] From The Four Handed Game by P.D.G.

Holmes immediately sensed my reluctance to join the two of them and he leapt up at once to encourage me to bring out my notebook and pencil and to pull up a chair close to that of our guest. My friend placated me with a cigar and I soon realised that Goldman had barely scratched the surface of the reason for his visit.

As if aware of my disapproval, Goldman greeted me with a mischievous smile and a tentative handshake.

"It is good to see you again, Doctor Watson, and I can assure you that you have missed absolutely nothing." Thankfully, Goldman often dispensed with his accent when in the presence of those that he trusted and the ensuing conversation became all the easier for me to transcribe as a consequence.

Once we were all settled, Holmes closed his eyes tightly and clasped his hands together, as if he were at prayer.

"Pray, describe to us the events and circumstances that have brought you to our door this morning. Remember to be as precise and concise with the details as you can, while omitting absolutely nothing of importance." Holmes requested.

"Well Mr. Holmes, the matter is simple enough in itself, but it is the circumstances of my discovery that have motivated me to come to seek your advice." Goldman moved forward to the edge of his seat as his excitement began to surface.

"As you know gentlemen, there are very few uncommon movements or discoveries of fine jewels and precious objects that occur, without my being made aware of them. Many of my more intimate associates are aware of my interest in those objects that do not necessarily find their way to the more respectable dealers or auctioneers, for a variety of different reasons. Consequently, my colleagues will alert me to their availability within a very short period of time, but with the utmost discretion, of course." Goldman cleared his throat, so that Holmes and I had been left in little doubt as to his true meaning. For my part, I did not really need any reminding of the true nature of Goldman's dubious profession and I buried myself in my notebook, to avoid having to meet the gaze of either of my companions.

Oblivious to my discomfort, our guest continued without any further ado.

"Therefore, I was most surprised when I received news of a huge and hitherto unknown treasure from a most uncommon source. An old friend of mine, who hails from the Greek Islands and shall remain nameless, unexpectedly arrived at my office one morning, in a state of great excitement. I knew at once that for him to make such a journey without prior word or warning could only mean one thing; he had obviously discovered an object of immense value. Naturally my anticipation was heightened still further, by the notion that there would be very little chance of any of my local competitors stealing a march on me on this; therefore, I made my friend feel very welcome indeed!"

Even my ever-tolerant friend raised an eyebrow at the mention of such skulduggery, but he invited Goldman to continue, nevertheless.

"Remember Watson, we are not here to judge, at least not at this point in our proceedings," Holmes explained.

Goldman greeted Holmes' pointed comment with a brief and furtive glance.

"Understandably, I was most disappointed to discover that my friend had an extensive knowledge of this treasure only, but remained clueless as to its present location," Goldman continued. "The haul is of an immense value and had recently been discovered by three Greek sponge divers in the depths of the Aegean Sea. My friend is in possession of very few other details, apart from the fact that this ancient and legendary treasure had been found amongst the wreckage of an ancient Roman vessel, which had once belonged to a great and noble general.

"Sadly any further information that the sponge divers might have possessed died with them, for they form the first in a long list of tragedies that have dogged anyone who had some connection to this great haul and the deadly and avaricious quest to claim its ownership. No doubt, Mr. Holmes, you will understand my request for absolute discretion, as I have no great desire for the same fate to befall either my friend or my good self," Goldman concluded anxiously.

"That is quite understandable; however, you have yet to impart to us any information of a tangible nature. I have no real use for the rumours and myths with which you have so far furnished us, and without any solid facts, even the deaths of the divers cannot positively be attached to the reclamation of this treasure," Holmes explained and not without a little agitation.

"Ah, but Mr. Holmes, you must understand that before I can feel able to divulge any further information to you, we must come to an arrangement. All I will tell you and with absolute confidence, is that my friend has been informed, by a most reliable source, of the imminent arrival of the treasure right here in the city of London, Indeed, a considerable portion of the haul might have arrived already, although it's exact whereabouts or intended destination still remains a complete mystery."

Holmes glanced across at me with an apologetic acknowledgment before responding to Goldman with a weary resignation.

"So, 'Rabbi' Goldman, what precisely is it that you propose?" Holmes asked with a feigned indifference.

"I hope that you will find it to be a straightforward and manageable enough arrangement Mr. Holmes. I suggest an uncomplicated exchange of information which I sincerely hope will prove to be to our mutual advantage. As soon as it falls into my hands, I shall bring you any news of the treasure's arrival and location, without a moment's hesitation. It goes without saying that should your own inquiries prove to be fruitful, I would expect you to also point me in the right direction."

Holmes now found it impossible to suppress an avalanche of laughter that had evidently been brewing within him for some time.

"Oh Goldman, while I can certainly understand how the results of my inquiries might prove to be of significant and material benefit to you, I fail to see what I might have to gain from such a prejudiced contract. I have no particular interest in obtaining an ancient treasure, nor do I see why you might have thought that I should have." I felt most gratified to hear my friend's objections, for I found the idea of cooperating with such a scoundrel to be abhorrent in the extreme.

"Granted that the treasure itself may not be of any real intrinsic value to you, Mr. Holmes, but I would have thought that the opportunity of grappling with a master poisoner and one who has already taken many innocent lives in the pursuit of wealth and self-preservation, would have proven to be something of a professional inducement to you," Goldman suggested mischievously.

Holmes' laughter subsided as suddenly as it had burst forth, and I was immediately consumed with indignation. I saw my friend's cheeks flush with excitement and as he lit a cigarette I recognised a fire in his eyes that I had witnessed on many such occasions in the past.

"Do you actually believe that the deaths of a group of sponge divers would be enough to induce me to fall in with your unsavoury little scheme?" Holmes asked expectantly.

"Oh I do, Mr. Holmes, although not for the sake of their deaths, but more for the manner of them. You see, the local police have come to the inescapable conclusion that each one of the victims had been murdered by the same master criminal, whose reputation in the region of the Eastern Mediterranean has been accruing on a daily basis. Alas, this individual's shadowy identity remains shrouded in mystery."

I was aghast to see that my friend was actually giving Goldman's scheme any credence or serious consideration. Holmes dwelt long and hard upon Goldman's proposal, and he stroked his long chin repeatedly with his thin, sinewy fingers.

"Have you anything tangible for me to work on at least? After all, so far you have presented me with nothing more than a collection of suggestions and hearsay. Would not your Hellenic friend be able to furnish me with just a few solid facts, which might at least form the basis of an investigation?" Holmes suggested.

"If only that were possible Mr. Holmes, but I am afraid that since our last meeting, which took place over dinner just three evenings ago, nothing more has been seen nor heard of him. I have put the word about amongst our mutual contacts and colleagues, but they all appear to be as mystified as I am as to his fate and present whereabouts," Goldman replied gravely.

"No doubt you fear that he has met the same fate as so many of his fellow countrymen," Holmes suggested.

"I do not know what to think, Mr. Holmes, but when you consider how ruthlessly anyone who has been in contact with this treasure has been dealt with so far, it is not hard to speculate upon a deadly fate for my poor friend," Goldman solemnly agreed. However, I had observed that all the while that he had been speaking; our devious friend had also been making a very obvious and deliberate attempt at removing an item from his inside pocket.

"Perhaps I do have something in my possession that might help you with your quest. However, you must understand that I have absolutely no intention of passing it over into your trust until you and I have reached a gentleman's agreement along the lines that I have previously described."

"I can promise you complete discretion and also my undertaking that this object will remain securely within my care. Beyond that I can assure you of nothing!" Holmes declared with not a little venom.

Goldman removed the object from his pocket with a resigned reluctance and he gradually revealed what appeared to have been an ancient and badly worn segment of parchment.

"When he handed it over to me, my friend could tell me very little about this unique object, other than the fact that the parchment had actually been found aboard the same wreck that had contained the treasure. He assured me that it had only survived the elements and the millennia by virtue of its having been wrapped in oilskin and placed within an airtight casket of bronze. I have been at my wits end, Mr. Holmes, because it is written in a very ancient form of the

47

Greek language that is unknown to my friend and indeed anyone else with whom he has consulted." Goldman concluded.

"It is from this that you expect me to be able to locate both your friend and your treasure and bring to justice a mysterious and murderous exponent of the dark art of the poison?" Holmes asked incredulously.

A resigned and despondent Menachem Goldman nodded his head solemnly and I was glad to see that he had begun to replace the parchment into his pocket as he rose to leave. I closed my notebook triumphantly and eagerly opened the door for our undesirable guest, who was now apparently prepared to accept the negative fate of his great plans.

To my great astonishment and dismay, Holmes suddenly ran over to the door and attempted to grab the parchment from our confused guest before it had disappeared once more into Goldman's pocket.

"The challenge is irresistible to me!" Holmes declared with a wild and irrepressible smile.

A much relived and astonished Goldman handed over the parchment without a moment's further hesitation, and he informed us that it was still possible to reach him at his old address. Both men had remained oblivious to my very obvious and understandable chagrin, although this had been diluted somewhat by my friend's departing warning to the grateful Menachem Goldman.

"I must remind you, Mr. Goldman that I promise you absolutely nothing!" Holmes slammed the door shut with a dramatic flourish and he immediately began to rub his hands together in a display of anticipation and great excitement.

I glanced up and observed the very obvious relish with which my friend had been welcoming his latest challenge and it was, therefore, with a grave reluctance, that I slowly reopened my notebook.

****

Chapter Four: The Historian

"In heaven's name Holmes, what can you possibly be thinking of?" Not for the first time, I began to berate my friend for having consorted and conspired with a man of such a dubious profession and unenviable reputation. However, my friend soon stopped me in my tracks by holding up an apologetic and conciliatory hand.

"Watson, the cause of your grievance is fairly obvious to me, not least due to the frosty manner that you had adopted towards our guest from the moment of his arrival. Nevertheless, you must have realised by now that in order to vanquish the devil it is occasionally necessary to consort with his minions," Holmes explained.

"Do you already consider this master of poison to be worthy of such a sinister and auspicious designation?"

"I most certainly do. When you consider that we know of at least four men who have lost their lives as a result of his quest for treasure and then bear in mind that his reputation has already begun to straddle the length and breadth of an entire continent, it must be acknowledged that here is an opponent worthy of our every deliberation and attention," Holmes replied with solemn intensity.

"Holmes, we know only of three deaths with any certainty." I queried.

"You are forgetting the fact that Goldman's friend from Greece had disappeared within days of passing on to him his scant knowledge of the treasure. It is, therefore, not unreasonable to suppose that this master of poison will stop at nothing in order to secure his aspirations and I am certain that Goldman's concerns for his friend's well-being are not without foundation."

All the while Holmes had been writing frantically at his desk and a moment later he called down to Mrs. Hudson in order that she might send off a wire for him with some urgency.

"I would hope that my colleague, Inspector Papadopoulos of the Athenian Police Department, might be able to shed some light upon the identity of Goldman's missing friend," Holmes responded to my questioning glance.

Upon handing over his draft, Holmes rather unceremoniously bundled our harassed landlady from the room, before outlining the next stage of his plan to me.

"In the absence of any further data at this time, we must now turn our attention towards an understanding of the contents of this parchment and the many secrets that it might contain. I should hope that you will not be too surprised Watson, were I to honour you with the unenviable task of completing this mission." Holmes smiled expectantly.

"I must apologise for my lack of insightfulness, but really Holmes, I fail to see how I can be of any real use in achieving that." I protested.

"Then kindly cast back your mind and you might recall the small matter of a rather ingenious code that had been disguised within the contents of a corrupted history of the life of Alexander the Great?" Holmes reminded me sarcastically.

"Well of course I remember that! That code had been the first of a very long line of bird crumbs that eventually led us to the Bavarian adventure."[6] I paused for a moment while I considered the implications of Holmes' reference. "You want me to enlist the services of Denbigh Grey, do you not?"

"If you would be so obliging." Holmes' raised eyebrow and an inclination of his head towards the door told me that I should depart without a moment's delay.

Consequently I was soon on my way to Bloomsbury, although I had almost forgotten my coat such had been my haste! Doubtless the dire conditions that had been prevailing outside would soon have brought me to a sharp halt and I pulled up my lapels gratefully as I set about my task.

I soon realised, with not a little consternation that my mission was going to prove to be no easy matter. I had been the last person to have met with Grey, just prior to my departure for Bavaria[7] and Holmes had quite naturally assumed, that I would know exactly where to find him, even after all this time. However, my friend had not realised that I had merely taken directions from a local library that Grey had frequented and I now found, to my dismay, that this establishment had been closed for the day!

---

[6] From the Illumination of Sherlock Holmes by PDG
[7] The Four Handed Game by PDG

Consequently, I had found myself wandering haphazardly through a veritable labyrinth of those large, red-bricked mansion houses that had been springing up everywhere over the last few decades. I recognised at once that there had been no distinguishing features to help me differentiate one building from the others, and my search appeared to be an endless and hopeless one.

Finally, once I had arrived at the very point of despair and surrender, I recognised the very same librarian, who had come to my aid on that previous occasion! He had been letting himself into one of those, aforementioned, mansion buildings, but my sharp footwork and an urgent call had prevented him from entering and disappearing from my view.

A few moments later and in a state of breathless elation, I found myself knocking upon the door of Denbigh Grey. While I had been standing there waiting for a response, I began to hear a succession of locks and bolts being thrown back and turned, as the timid historian set about the task of cautiously opening his door. A security chain had ensured that the door could not be pushed back beyond the safety of a narrow crack. However, the reception I then received upon being recognised, took me by complete surprise.

"Go away!" The diminutive scholar snapped aggressively, and I nearly lost a finger when he slammed the door shut!

On reflection his reaction should not have been an entirely unexpected one. After all, his life had been under the greatest threat the last time that he had been involved with Holmes and me, and the three years that had passed since, had clearly done little in diluting the nervous man's sense of dread at the mere sight of me.

I called through the heavy oak door repeatedly until the thin crack had reluctantly reappeared and Denbigh Grey finally relented and gave me the opportunity to at least explain the reason for my latest visit. He calmed down appreciatively when I told him of the source of the parchment and he then became quite animated once he had realised how old the document must have been.

I had clearly whetted Grey's appetite but he went on to explain that he was now settled in for the evening, although I suspected that his nature made him wary of going out of doors at such an hour. Nevertheless he did promise to come to Baker Street the following morning and although I was returning to Holmes empty-handed and without having actually seen the man fully, I had been quietly confident of a successful conclusion to my endeavour.

I had been greatly relieved to see that Denbigh Grey proved to be as good as his word and he had arrived at Baker Street just a few moments after our breakfast things had been cleared away. I had gone to great length in explaining to Holmes the nature of Grey's nervous disposition and my friend promised to be at his very best behaviour. In that I was not to be disappointed.

"Good morning Mr. Grey and I must say that it is good of you to come at such a short notice. Perhaps I might arrange a cup of coffee for you?" Holmes' tone was soft and quite welcoming, so much so in fact that Grey seemed to be put completely at ease and he accepted the offer of coffee without a moment's hesitation.

Holmes' tone had not been quite so modulated when he had called down for the coffee, but Mrs. Hudson responded promptly if somewhat reluctantly. Holmes waited a moment for the little historian to take a sip or two from his drink, before slowly bringing into view the reason for Grey's visit; the ancient parchment.

Denbigh Grey received this treasure with a slow and careful reverence, while at the same time barely managing to suppress a feverish excitement. To our great surprise, Grey had been able to read through and translate the document in no time at all. However, he then decided to withhold his conclusions until he had repeated the process and confirmed his findings to himself. He gulped down the remainder of his coffee and swallowed hard before imparting his conclusions to us.

Finally Grey managed to compose himself and gather his thoughts.

"Oh gentlemen, I do apologise if my findings disappoint you, but this document does not refer to a treasure in the traditional sense of the word at all. However, to someone of my own particular turn of mind it tells of an object of immense value." Grey caressed the manuscript as if it had been his dearest pet or child and there had been no trace of regret on his face as he finally explained his findings.

I smiled maliciously to myself as I thought of the avaricious designs of Menachem Goldman and his lust for a glorious and wondrous fortune. Furthermore, as Grey's account continued I realised that Goldman's dreams were progressively turning to nought.

"Gentlemen, we have here a brief, but surprisingly detailed description of an object that has long been thought of as mythical and to some, almost impossible to conceive of, the Antikythera Mechanism!" Grey made this proclamation as if this mechanism had been the most sought after and famed object in the world. However, just one glance at our faces had been enough to convince the historian that a more elaborate explanation had been sorely needed.

"You should not berate yourselves unduly gentlemen, for I can assure you that there are very few people, outside of those with a most singular field of interest, who have even heard of the 'Mechanism,' much less have an understanding of its functions." Grey set upon his testimony with what can best be described as great relish.

"In the briefest and most simplistic terms, the Antikythera Mechanism is nothing less than an incredibly advanced and sophisticated analogue calculator, whose designs were millennia ahead of its time! It boasted literally dozens of intermeshed gears and exquisitely worked cogwheels, which surpassed those of even the very finest of our contemporary time pieces.

Of course our limited understanding of the complexities of the mechanism makes it impossible for us to fathom its capabilities and potential. However, there are many archaeologists who are convinced that the

'Antikythera Mechanism' could calculate not only the movements of the sun and moon, but also those of the other planets within our solar system. Some have even speculated that it could actually trace the progress of the galaxy itself!"

Grey had been rendered breathless by this time, although Holmes had been left as nonplussed as I would have expected him to have been. Hopefully Holmes would not mind me mentioning here that at our first time of meeting, he had actually confessed to being indifferent to and ignorant of the fact that the Earth orbited around the sun, rather than the other way around!

Naturally I did not pass on this humiliating secret to our guest who now proceeded to explain that the parchment had undoubtedly been a mere fragment of the manifest from the treasure ship of the great Roman General, Lucullus.

As Grey continued to explain the significant role that Lucullus had played in the destruction of Rome's greatest enemy of the time, namely Mithradates VI, the King of ancient Pontus, I was surprised to observe that Holmes had become enthralled by Grey's tales of this enigmatic King and his ultimate destruction by an inexorable power. Undoubtedly the "mechanism" had been part of an enormous cache that had been plundered from the treasure house of Mithradates, but to any student of history it was surely of a far greater importance and value than any number of lustrous jewels.

However, it was only once Grey had made mention of the "Mithradate," a legendary universal antidote associated with the king, that my friend became suddenly animated. He leant forward in his chair and entreated our guest to continue with such an enthusiasm that the historian seemed to be quite taken aback by my friend's behaviour. Grey hesitated for a moment or two and swallowed hard before venturing to persist with his explanation.

"You see gentlemen, as a young man Mithradates had been subjected to the awful experience of witnessing the death of several of his closest family members by means of deadly poison. Consequently, during the course of a brief, but self-imposed, exile, which occurred during his formative years, the young king set about ensuring that he did not meet with a similar fate upon his return.

"By consuming as many toxins as he had been able to locate, Mithradates had managed to develop immunity to each of them, eventually transforming this unique gift into an infallible and universal antidote. Indeed, his antitoxin had proved to be so successful that at the time of his inevitable destruction, Mithradates had failed in each of his attempts at poisoning himself! As a final and desperate resort the doomed King persuaded his faithful servants to take his life for him, with the thrust of a sword."

By now I had convinced myself that in this rebellious and eccentric ancient king, Holmes had recognised a kindred spirit and that his fascination with this subject extended beyond the mere mention of the word poison, despite its relevance to our current investigation.

"Tell me Mr. Grey, have you been able to translate and identify this antitoxin from within the contents of this text?" Holmes asked with an unabated enthusiasm.

"Unfortunately that part of the text is so complex and technical that I shall require many hours of detailed analysis before I will be able to unlock its secrets. As to the treasure itself.......well those mysterious baubles probably still lie within the depths of the Aegean Sea." He concluded.

"In that case, you will have very little time to waste Mr. Grey!"

To the consternation of Denbigh Grey, Holmes suddenly leapt up and while thrusting the parchment into the little man's trembling hand, he bundled him towards the door. I tried to calm and placate the nervous historian with an apologetic and placating hand on his shoulder and as I led him to the front door I managed to coax from him a promise that he would report any progress that he might make as urgently as he possibly could.

By the time that I had climbed the stairs, Holmes had already returned to his chair with a lighted pipe and his tightly closed eyes indicated an hour or two of silent contemplation.

****

Chapter Five: The Tides of Death

As one might imagine, the remainder of my day passed very slowly indeed, and I soon discovered that, even once Holmes had roused himself from his meditative contemplations, he remained disappointingly reluctant to discuss the visit of Denbigh Grey and its potential consequences.

Therefore, I decided to retire to my own room and leave my friend to his pipe and his thoughts. I took a glass of port and my current reading material with me, but it was not long before the effects of both the drink and a very long and boring book had lulled me into a deep and restful sleep.

I was awoken just before dawn, by a very familiar sight: that of my friend Sherlock Holmes leaning over me with a cigarette trailing from his lips and a glint of excitement in his eyes. I must admit that I did not greet this interruption in the gladdest of spirits and my mood had been darkened still further by the constant prodding of his fingers to which Holmes had been subjecting my shoulder.

"Watson, Watson, you really must dress at once, the journey begins!" Holmes beamed, and his enthusiasm forced me to slowly open my eyes.

Naturally, I hurriedly went about my toilet and as I joined my friend in the dining room. I soon realised that I had barely enough time to consume a small cup of coffee and a slice of toast if we were to catch our train. Therefore, it was only once we had been seated aboard our carriage that Holmes deigned to explain the reason for our urgent departure for Westgate-on-Sea, in Kent.

He pulled out a wire that he had received that morning and perhaps sensing my disgruntled disposition, Holmes adopted his most charming of tones.

"My dear Watson, I offer you a thousand apologies for my boorish and untimely intrusion, but as you can see the matter is of the utmost moment."

I took up the wire, which had come from our old friend Inspector Stanley Hopkins and my attention had been immediately drawn to his request that we should "arrive before the turning of the tide!" otherwise, the wire had been most scant of detail and therefore, we had much to speculate upon as we made our way towards the Kentish coast.

"So Watson, what are we supposed to make of this most oblique summons?" Holmes asked while offering me one of his cigarettes.

"Well, there really is very little for us to go on," I agreed with an ironic laugh. "Nevertheless, I am sure that by now you are already half ways towards solving the case!" I added with unnecessary sarcasm.

"Now Watson, I suppose I do deserve such a churlish response from you, but surely there is enough here for us to suppose that a very intriguing investigation lies ahead of us. For example, every summons that we have received from Inspector Hopkins thus far, has resulted in a case worthy enough of your literary attention, have they not?"

"He has certainly never wasted our time with a dull and routine inquiry and as I recall, each one of his cases has always involved that touch of the outré which you have always found to be so appealing." I conceded. "Besides which, he emphatically states here that 'we shall not consider it to be a futile journey.' However, he does not explain why the turning of the tide is of so much importance to him."

"As you know Watson, I am seldom drawn towards the folly of mere speculation, but I should not be too far off the mark were I to suppose that there is an object on the beach that we need to examine before the onset of the rising tide. I say object, but there is very little than cannot be safely removed, save for the scene of a crime." Holmes stopped from actually naming the crime, but his features tightened into the gravest of representations.

"Do you think it to be a case of murder?" I asked quietly.

"I think it not unlikely," Holmes replied with a pensive reluctance and he pursed his lips with his right forefinger.

Despite the very obvious excitement that my friend had been suppressing throughout much of the journey, he remained surprisingly silent and had refused to be drawn further towards any redundant conjecture. We had been passing through some of the most delightful Kent countryside that you could imagine, but the dark brown autumnal hues were as much of a reflection of our moods as a depiction of the time of year. Holmes maintained his silence throughout, but I could sense a mounting thrill and anticipation building within him as we drew ever closer to our destination.

We pulled into our station at precisely the scheduled hour and when Holmes checked his timepiece he appeared to have been satisfied with his findings. We were much relieved to have discovered that the shoreline at Westgate was but a brisk walk from the station, for there were no traps or carts to be had for neither love nor money. The porter gave us some simple directions and we had been reassured to discover that the incoming tide made a very slow advancement along this stretch of coast. Nevertheless we were determined to make as fast a progress as possible and in just a few minutes, having traversed the small level crossing, a wide stretch of grey open sea loomed before us.

The broad expanse of golden sand was bordered by a stone promenade above which stood the imposing, red bricked St. Mildred's Hotel which bore the name of this particular bay. Apart from a square wooden kiosk, which had been shuttered up for the approaching winter and a small group of men standing in the centre of the beach, the whole place had been completely deserted. At that moment it had been hard to imagine the teeming throngs of people who normally gathered there upon the promenade, at the height of summer.

As we drew ever closer, a strong and penetrative wind picked up from the Channel and we both pulled up our coat lapels as we made our descent onto the damp, soft sand. Before too long we had been able to make out the familiar shape of Stanley Hopkins. Even though Hopkins had been standing in the centre of a small group of his officers, he had been easily distinguishable by virtue of his height. As soon as he had recognised us, Hopkins greeted us with a long and expansive wave and we could sense his urgency as he directed his men to maintain a complete circle while he stepped forward to greet us.

"Mr. Holmes and Dr. Watson, I cannot express my gratitude and relief at seeing you arrive at such a timely moment," Hopkins exclaimed while shaking us both most heartily by the hand. He pointed towards the human circle in front of us and by now we could make out, quite clearly, the body of a man, who had been surprisingly bereft of both coat and jacket, lying in its centre.

"So it is a case of murder then?" I asked.

"I cannot really say that with any certainty Doctor. As you can see, nobody has been allowed close to the body, from the time of its discovery until now."

"What were the exact circumstances of the discovery?" To my surprise Holmes expressed no great desire to examine the body with any urgency, for he casually lit a cigarette while awaiting the Inspector's reply. Then I realised that the large grey rock pools, that seemed to guard each side of the beach, had only just started to fill up with water and that we had time enough.

"An elderly resident of the St. Mildred's Hotel was out walking his dog along the promenade, shortly after dawn this morning." Hopkins pointed towards the imposing edifice that we had just passed. "The dog walker could only confirm that the man on the beach had been showing no sign of life or movement and he immediately returned to the hotel to raise the alarm. From there, the hotel manager despatched one of his pages to go in search of the police. Between then and now, nobody has been near to the body apart from me," Hopkins replied definitively.

Holmes nodded his appreciation. "Inspector Hopkins, what were your initial conclusions?"

"Well, I could see no traces in the sand between the body and the waterline, so I can only conclude that the body had been washed ashore by the previous tide. As you can see the gentleman has lost some of his upper garments. Perhaps he had even removed them himself, in an effort to lower his weight in the water, while he had been struggling. There are no marks of violence that I can see, so my initial hypothesis was that he had died of a misadventure at sea. However....." The Inspector's voice tailed off as he became lost in his own thoughts.

My friend threw away his cigarette impatiently and his eyes sparkled when he realised that there had been much more to this incident than there had first appeared.

"Remember Inspector that even the smallest and most inconsequential detail might yet prove to be of the greatest significance," Holmes reminded him.

"I cannot, for the life of me, reconcile the fact that the body is almost dry. I know that the tides around these parts are somewhat sluggish, twelve hours in fact between high and low, but even so, at this time of year you would expect there to be considerably more dampness about his clothing, especially around his waistband or his shoes and socks."

"You would indeed, Inspector; and it is gratifying to note that you have certainly done your homework." Hopkins was visibly gratified by Holmes' sincere compliment.

"Furthermore, there are a variety of footprints around the body, which I have kept clear for your examination, that put paid to my initial theory I think. However, it is the presence of these objects I found in the dead man's trouser pocket, which prompted me to send for you, Mr. Holmes. To my mind, they are simply inexplicable!" Hopkins exclaimed and Holmes extended his eager hands.

Once he had scanned and then passed them over for my perusal, I soon realised that these objects were an indecipherable letter, which had been written in modern Greek and a railway ticket from Victoria Station to Ramsgate, a large harbour town located further along the same line. My friend appeared to have been as mystified as the inspector by these discoveries, but then we all became aware of a noticeable acceleration in the approaching tide and so we abandoned any further discussion until after we had examined the body.

At Holmes' request, Hopkins ordered his men to move carefully away from the site and while Holmes scrutinised the surrounding area, I bent over the body. At first glance, I could find nothing that contradicted Hopkins' appraisal. However, once I had rolled back the dead man's shirt sleeves, I notice a large and unusual puncture mark in his lower left arm.

My further examination also realised an excess of saliva around the mouth, indications of severe muscle paralysis and unusually dilated pupils. I became convinced that any further examination, especially under laboratory conditions, would conclude that the man had been injected with a lethal dose of hemlock! This surprised me somewhat, as it was a poison more commonly used in parts of Europe and North Africa, where the deadly plant is far easier to come by.

However, I had no time to pass on my findings to my companions, as the sea was edging ever closer, and Holmes' examinations were becoming more urgent and frenetic. I could see Hopkins' agitation increasing, so we were both much relieved when Holmes finally leapt back onto his feet in triumph!

"Inspector Hopkins, I suggest that you arrange for the removal of the body, with little or no delay!" He called as he pointed towards and then moved away from the accelerating waves.

It was then, to everyone's surprise, that Holmes suddenly broke away from our progress to the promenade and began to crawl on his hands and knees along an entirely different path. Although inexplicable to the rest of us, Holmes' strange behaviour produced great excitement in my friend. The occasional cry of satisfaction and a broad smile upon his face, at the conclusion of his extraordinary exercise, certainly confirmed my hypothesis.

Hopkins summoned his men to return immediately and by the time that we three had climbed back onto the promenade and removed all traces of the beach from our clothing; the dead man was already on his way to the local coroner's mortuary. We stood there in silence for a few moments, while Holmes looked to me for the results of my examination. At the same time, Hopkins and I had stared at my friend for an explanation.

The incoming tide had, by now, produced a strengthening of the accompanying wind, and we all looked towards the hotel as a suitable place for shelter and comfortable deliberation. For my part, I longed for a means of supplementing the brief and meagre meal that I had bolted down prior to our hurried departure from Baker Street earlier that day.

We found the landlord at the St. Mildred's Hotel to be a most genial and accommodating gentleman, whose ruddy complexion told of many years spent by the sea. After a lunch of steak and kidney pie and a pint of ale, we settled down in front of a welcoming fire with our pipes and a glass of cognac. Holmes and Hopkins had both been impressed with and fascinated by the conclusions of my examination, and Hopkins promised to confirm their validity once the Coroner had completed his examination. Then Hopkins and I leant back into our chairs in excited anticipation of the outcome of my friend's assessment.

"I really must congratulate you both, for having made my task so much easier than it might have been. To you, Inspector Hopkins for having maintained such a clean and methodical crime scene, thereby enabling me to identify the exact circumstances of all that had occurred. I must also thank you Watson for your concise and enlightening examination of the body and for your findings.

Of course, I would expect nothing less from my stalwart man of medicine!" Holmes' praise was like music to my ears, for his appraisal of some of my previous contributions, had not always been quite as complimentary.

"So, now to my own humble input, for there is little doubt in my mind as to the true passage of events." Hopkins had shared my look of surprise, for having already dismissed the theory that the body had been washed ashore, my view of things was as oblique as it had been before, apart from the obvious fact that the man had indeed been poisoned.

Holmes had not been unmindful of our very obvious state of confusion and initially our ignorance seemed to be a source of puzzlement, even amusement, to him.

"Although obvious to me, I forget that neither of you have been privy to the footprints in the sand, nor to the most singular revelations to which they have led me. I can tell you, with absolute certainty, that apart from the unfortunate victim, there had been three other men there on the beach with him!" Ignoring our open-mouthed amazement and disbelief, Holmes continued with his customary enthusiasm and gusto.

"Oh yes, of that I am in little doubt. As soon as I had dismissed the obvious traces of Hopkins', round toed boots, I had been able to recognise three other sets of prints. One set came from a very expensive pair of evening shoes, which had left a very faint impression and that skirted around the perimeter of the crime scene. The other two belonged to identical sets of heavy, square toed boots that had sunk far deeper into the sand than those of the evening shoes, almost as if the boot wearers had been sharing a considerable weight. Naturally, I concluded that the evening shoes belonged to the director of the operation and that the deep-set boots had been worn by his henchman, who had been tasked with carrying the body onto the beach."

"So you are convinced that the gentleman was dead even before he arrived here?" Hopkins asked quietly.

"If not dead, then he was very close to death. Watson, unless my memory fails me, I believe that hemlock can be a very slow-acting poison."

"Of course, that depends on the dosage, but in the hands of a skilled practitioner it certainly can be," I confirmed.

"Excellent! Then my theory can be borne out by the facts." Holmes rubbed his hands together excitedly; as if he had just been presented with an unattainable and cherished gift.

"Gentlemen, it is my belief that the victim had been followed upon his journey from the very moment that his train had pulled out in London. Shortly afterward he would have fallen into the company of the three men from the beach and then once ingratiated by them, he had been plied with drinks from the buffet car saloon.

It was then that the poison would have been applied and the poor fellow had then been helped from the train in a state of incapacitation. No doubt our villains had gone to great lengths to ensure that the staff and perhaps the other passengers within the buffet car had witnessed this copious consumption of alcohol, thereby providing them with a quite innocent explanation for their companion's sorry condition.

"It would have been far easier for them to have disposed of the body unobserved upon the deserted beach here in Westgate than in the busier port town of Ramsgate. Obviously, this would explain why the ticket was still in the dead man's possession, when you found him, for it was never destined to be redeemed at his intended destination.

I would also commend to your attention the lack of ripples in the sand." Holmes added enticingly in his usual inscrutable manner and he smiled to himself while he lit a cigarette.

Hopkins and I exchanged glances of confusion, which did not go unnoticed by my friend. However, instead of clarifying his previous statement, he continued along a quite different tangent.

"Not surprisingly, the men in question did not possess your detailed knowledge of the local conditions, Inspector Hopkins, and therefore they assumed that at some point the sea would simply wash away the evidence, if not the body itself. In either event, but for my timely intervention, your initial, although quite understandable, perception of events would have become the accepted one."

"Surely they would have feared being observed during such a clandestine and laborious undertaking?" I asked.

"Undoubtedly Watson, but see the time at which the train ticket had been issued. By the hour of their arrival here in Westgate, it would have been quite dark, especially at this time of year and they would have felt far more secure of remaining undetected." Holmes explained while producing the dead man's travel document for my perusal.

"Now I understand and yet you have failed to explain the importance that you seem to attach to the ripples in the sand, or rather to the lack of them." I reminded him.

"Oh Watson, you see, yet you do not observe. Did you not notice how a portion of the old wooden water break had been deliberately broken away? Furthermore, the fact that the motion of the incoming waves had created a series of geometric ripples in the soft, moist sand, has also seemed to have escaped your notice. The point being, that the area of sand around the dead man's body had been deliberately rendered as quite flat and smooth and therefore out of character with the rest of the beach. Evidently, this action had been our mysterious gang's final and spontaneous attempt at obscuring their traces."

"I do not understand Mr. Holmes, for when I examined the site myself, I could make out very little in the way of footprints." The puzzled inspector protested.

"Very likely not Inspector, for the perpetrators of this crime had come very close to totally obscuring them with the plank. However, to a trained observer, there were still vague, but visible outlines of each man's shoes, which they had evidently failed to have noticed. Obviously, without any further examination, I had not been able to identify them with any certainty.

"As you know Watson, there is a perfectly sound reason behind everything that I do. As a consequence, my strange cavorting across the sand, as you might have seen and regarded it, resulted in the confirmation of my initial notion. Obviously the boot prints, which had been made on the return trip to the promenade, were not nearly as pronounced or as deep as they had been on their outward journey and this had been due to the lack of that excess weight."

"Well upon my word!" Hopkins exclaimed before letting out a low whistle of amazement. "Great thought and planning had evidently gone into this crime."

"No, Inspector, quite the contrary I would say. I should rather call it quick thinking and ruthless improvisation. They had been determined, possibly even desperate, to prevent the man from reaching his intended destination, regardless of the consequences. I should imagine that the ferry from Ramsgate to Ostend was to have been the man's next stage of a long journey back to Greece."

"As usual Holmes, your reasoning is as remarkable as it is pure. Each one of your discoveries have undoubtedly corroborated your every hypothesis." I confirmed with great excitement.

"Yes Watson, it all fits!"

"That is all very well, yet we are still no closer to knowing the identity of any of the parties, nor indeed the motive for such a singular crime." Hopkins quite rightly pointed out.

"You are undoubtedly correct Inspector, but in order to procure that information I shall have to return to London to further my inquiries."

Without warning, Holmes squeezed my arm with such intensity that I had almost been prone to cry out in pain. He must have sensed that I had been on the point of mentioning Menachem Goldman's missing friend, who had also hailed from Greece. In that, my friend had been quite correct and once I realised that he had his own good reasons for withholding that information from the Inspector, I held my peace without hesitation.

We all rose to leave the sanctuary of the hotel lounge with a grave reluctance, for the dire weather outside had been showing very little sign of relenting. With an unnecessary gallantry, Hopkins decided to walk with us to the station. During the course of our harried journey, Holmes and Hopkins pledged an exchange of information with each other, as and when it became available.

We arrived at Westgate station with only a few moments to spare before the arrival of the London bound train.

****

Chapter Six: The Warning

I am ashamed to admit that, throughout the vast majority of the two-hour journey back to Victoria, I had inadvertently fallen into a deep and dreamless sleep.

A combination of my premature awakening that morning, the excitement of our discoveries during the day, together with the heady sea air, had rendered my attempts at staying awake impossible. I was embarrassed to see my friend's amusement at my plight, so I mumbled a hasty apology just as our train was pulling into the London terminus.

"Oh Watson, you should not trouble yourself, for as you know, I am quite often more comfortable with my own company." I could not help but laugh at yet another example of Holmes' egocentric nature and then I began to feel insulted, despite myself.

Due to the lateness of the hour, it was with a great deal of persuasive charm that I eventually managed to coax a late supper from our disgruntled and reluctant landlady. I devoured this makeshift meal most heartily and then, after a last pipe and a glass of port, I made my way up to my room. My friend had been strangely quiet, since our return and I left him in his chair in a state of deep contemplation, where I was sure he would remain for goodness knows how long.

Therefore, it had been with some surprise when I had discovered that Holmes had evidently risen long before

I had done and I found him to be waiting impatiently for me by the fire, while I completed my breakfast.

"So Watson, what are we to make of our work on the Kent coast yesterday?" Holmes asked eagerly while rubbing his hands together in front of the fire.

"Well, there certainly seems to be little doubt now as to the fate of Goldman's friend from Greece." I asserted while deliberately rubbing the area of my arm that Holmes had so painfully pinched while we had been in the company of Inspector Hopkins. Naturally, this had not gone unnoticed by my friend.

"My sincere apologies Watson for any injury that I might have caused you, but you must understand that it is absolutely vital that this knowledge remains within our exclusive domain, or at least until such time as I have a clearer perception of how things really stand. Remember our adversary is not only highly skilled in the arts of poison, but he is also ruthless in pursuing his objective. What better way has he of assuming the title of the 'Poison King' than by rendering himself immune to his own lethal weaponry?" Holmes concluded gravely.

"I understand, but surely Hopkins might have proved to be useful in helping us pursue our inquiries?"

"Sadly no, for there is very little that any of us can do until we either hear from Menachem Goldman, Denbigh Grey, or my colleague in Athens. Although, unbeknown to any of them, we do have one slight advantage over them all: namely, the identity of the Poison King!" Holmes proclaimed, while slowly extracting the sorry remains of a calling card from within his jacket pocket.

The card had been severely damaged by the elements and therefore barely legible and I was aghast once I had realised that Holmes had extracted this from the dead man's body without Hopkins' knowledge. Now I understood Holmes' violent objection to my illuminating Hopkins still further and my past experience told me that to admonish Holmes, for withholding vital evidence, would prove to be a total waste of time!

The information on the card had been sparse yet sufficient and I could just make out the name: Count Dragos and the fact that he was an international collector of fine arts.

"Well, at least we can now put a name to our enemy, if not a face. I assume that you are in little doubt of the fact that the dead man is indeed Goldman's missing friend?" I asked.

"Unless one of the dead sponge divers suddenly came back to life in order to deposit himself on a beach in Kent, then yes, I would say so! We have the letter written in Greek and his neck medallion is one, typical of that region. Furthermore, we must also consider his dark complexion and this after his body having endured so much, before and after his death. It cannot simply be a succession of coincidences." Holmes insisted.

However, before I could delve even deeper into my friend's thought processes and conclusions, we suddenly became aware of a commotion coming from the hallway below followed by the alarmed voice of Mrs. Hudson.

"No gentlemen, you cannot simply barge you way upstairs unannounced!" She cried.

Nevertheless, a resounding vibration upon the stairs indicated that Mrs. Hudson had been somewhat less than successful with her remonstrations and a moment later the door to our room was flung open with considerable force. Holmes rose quickly to confront our uninvited guests and appeared to be rather surprised to find only one man standing there before him.

"Will your friend not be joining us?" Holmes asked pointedly, to which our guest had responded with a raised, questioning eyebrow.

"I am certain that I have been living here long enough to be able to recognise the sound of two sets of boots ascending the stairs." Holmes explained in a dismissive and disparaging tone.

"Of course, but my colleague will remain just outside the door for reasons, shall we say, of discretion."

The man standing before us was tall and heavily built, but his manner and stature exuded both strength and not a little menace. He was dressed immaculately in a plain black suit and tie with a white shirt and a pair of strong black boots. He was rather dark of complexion and sported two-day stubble upon his face. Although his English was exact and perfectly pronounced, he spoke with an accent that was of a distinctly Slavic origin, possibly Romanian.

Despite our guest's intention to intimidate, Sherlock Holmes appeared to be entirely relaxed in his response to him, almost jovial, in fact, as he stood there face to face with him, close to the door.

"I would offer you a seat, but I have absolutely no intention of allowing this interview to continue for more than exactly two minutes. Therefore, might I suggest that you state your intention as briefly as possible?" Holmes said with a threatening grimace.

The man had been clearly taken aback by my friend's aggressive attitude and subsequently took his advice without a moment's consideration.

"Very well then, it has come to our attention that a certain treasure has only recently come into your possession. Our client believes that he has a prior claim......."

"Ah, so there is a third party involved! Perhaps he is awaiting the outcome on the street below?" Holmes asked with an ironic smile.

The man ignored Holmes' flippancy and he continued without pause, evidently taking my friend at his word.

"Our client believes that he has a prior claim to the treasure's ownership and wishes it to be returned to him without delay. Naturally we would not consider the prospect of you making such a sacrifice without our compensating you, to a certain degree." The man added with an unconvincing smile.

"That is indeed most generous of your client." Holmes could barely suppress a smile as he replied. "However, I must point out that there exists one small problem which you may not have considered. You should know at once that I am not in possession of that or any other type of treasure. Furthermore, I do not even know of the whereabouts of any such haul."

"That is most unfortunate for you, Mr. Holmes. Our client has been informed otherwise and I can assure you that he will stop at nothing in order to obtain that which is rightfully his." The threat had been issued calmly and quietly, but that did nothing to diminish its menace.

Once again I had been consumed by the inclination to inform our unwanted visitor of our findings upon Westgate beach and the dire consequences to him and his colleagues of our having made such a discovery. Thankfully, the bruise on my arm, which I had received earlier, told me to maintain my silence. Nevertheless, Holmes already knew the name of the client, and if he had felt the need to withhold that knowledge, it was certainly not for me to do otherwise.

Holmes responded to this warning with a silent stare and proceeded to examine his timepiece with an obvious deliberation.

"I see, well then, I have to inform you that unless we see your proposal in the agony columns of either The Times or The Daily Telegraph, within the next forty eight hours, we shall set about retrieving the treasure regardless of your willingness to cooperate." The man made this statement as a matter fact rather than conjecture.

"Perhaps you could inform us of the precise nature of this treasure?" Holmes suggested. "After all, you can hardly expect me to produce something of which I have no prior knowledge or description."

"That is surely your concern, Mr. Holmes, not ours. I have merely informed you of the price you would have to pay should you fail to comply. Besides, I do believe that my two minutes have now come to an end." With a most sinister smile and without another word, the man turned smartly on his heels and a moment later we could hear two sets of boots clattering down the stairs.

To my great surprise, there had been no indication from my friend, that this encounter had left him in any way perturbed or concerned. Indeed, if anything, it had had the exact opposite effect upon him. He rubbed his hands together excitedly and almost jigged over to the mantelpiece, from where he took down his Persian slipper and the old clay pipe that he used at times of consideration.

"So Watson, the disparate strands of this little matter, undoubtedly seem to be coming together very nicely, would you not say?" Holmes asked jovially.

"Our lives have just been threatened by an international gang, whom we now know will stop at nothing in achieving their goal and we have been asked to produce a treasure about which we have no prior knowledge, save for the vague proposition of Menachem Goldman. So I should hardly refer to it as a 'little matter'!" I exclaimed. "Besides which, I fail to see how the strands are coming together. Quite the opposite, I should say, for to me the waters have been muddied still further by that untimely visit."

"Oh Watson, surely you will have noticed the distinctly Slavic flavour to the man's accent and is not Dragos a name that resonates with that particular region? Besides, you must have observed the faint residue of Kentish sand that still clings to the heel of that man's boot" Holmes asked incredulously.

"I must admit that I did not, however, had I done so, I should surely have immediately identified him as being one of the culprits on the beach! What I fail to reconcile is the fact that armed with that knowledge, you have simply allowed him to leave here unhindered!" For once, I had been at a loss as to my friend's reasoning and inaction.

"Watson, the two men here today are merely pawns in the employ of this self-styled king of poisons. Although complicit in the murder on the beach, I do not think that either of them is capable of such a deadly skill. I am certain that if we had apprehended either one or even both of them, Count Dragos' plans would have been merely postponed, but not annulled. Besides which, we have been given forty-eight hours in which to bring our own plans to fruition. For now, however, we shall simply have to wait for the replies to my wires."

I recoiled at the very thought of such a scenario, for if I had learned only one thing about the nature of Sherlock Holmes, it was his inability to wait and maintain his patience.

I was in very little doubt that the next forty-eight hours were going to prove to be most fraught indeed.

****

Chapter Seven: The Sword of Damocles

Mercifully, Holmes' descent into a series of erratic and fluctuating moods which I had so dreaded and which had usually been borne of his frustration, did not manifest itself for as long as I had feared or anticipated.

The absence of communications from both Menachem Goldman and Denbigh Grey was offset somewhat by the arrival of a reply from Holmes' Athenian colleague, Inspector Papadopoulos. When it finally arrived on the following morning, Holmes tore it open with a feverish anticipation. Then, with an obvious disdain, he ushered Mrs. Hudson from the room, despite her best attempts at clearing away our breakfast things.

I observed that the communication had been an unusually lengthy one and Holmes read through its entirety with great deliberation before deciding to inform me of its contents.

"Although well-intentioned, the first part of this missive is very much a repetition of Denbigh Grey's summary and therefore superfluous to our needs. Inspector Papadopoulos has confirmed that our friend, Count Dragos, is indeed rumoured to be a practitioner in the art of poisoning and that the fear of his name has spread far and wide due to the deadly effect of his practise. His notorious reputation extends from the Slavic states to Greece itself and the Inspector goes on to elaborate upon the legend of Mithradates' attempted suicide and his invention and use of the much sought after 'Universal Antidote'.

"That much we already knew. However, one question that has been nagging at me since the inception of this case is the reason behind Dragos' obsessive desire to obtain the secrets of this universal antidote. After all, it is rare for an assassin to be desirous of a cure for his victims. Would a conventional killer seek a way of safely removing a bullet from his latest target?" Holmes proposed.

"No, indeed not, although if Dragos really aspires to be known as the undisputable, contemporary poison king, it is not inconceivable that he should strive to be the true master of his craft," I speculated.

"Not inconceivable, but it is highly unlikely that he should bring such unnecessary attention upon himself in order to obtain something for which he has very little real need. Our visitor of yesterday seemed to have little doubt that his master was prepared to go to any lengths in order to obtain the object of his quest." Holmes replied.

"Perhaps, but the man did not actually indicate a specific item from the treasure that his 'client' wished to acquire. For all we know he really does have a passion for fine objects and lustrous jewels and that his quest for the 'Mithradate' is pure speculation on our part." Even as I spoke, I could sense from my friend's manner that the secret that we had been debating was within the wire that he was still clutching like a prize. Holmes slowly lit his pipe while he formulated his reply.

"Watson, I must admit that it has not even occurred to me that there has to be a very good reason for Dragos remaining at large, despite his having accrued such a deadly reputation. That he is a master of his craft is beyond dispute, yet it is hard to believe that someone with such a status has, thus far, evaded the arm of the law. Nevertheless, the answer to this conundrum does seem to lie within this wire." Holmes declared while waving the sheet.

I could not comprehend why Holmes had decided to engage me in this debate, when the answers to his queries had been within his grasp all along and I told him so.

"Watson, it may well have seemed like a futile exercise to you, but then you have grossly underestimated the value of a good sounding board to the trained logician. Much of my work takes place within my mind, but the importance of being able to vocalise it to a receptive set of ears cannot be too highly emphasised. Therefore, your inadvertent contribution is of the greatest value to me." Holmes added, as a means of placating me, although he had seemed oblivious to the very evident, though unintended, insult that he had afforded me.

"That is all very well, but perhaps you could now explain to me the reasoning behind Dragos' obsession with the 'Mithradate'?" I asked curtly.

"It is for the very same reason that he has so far evaded prosecution. Watson, his felony is perhaps unique within the annals of crime! Inspector Papadopoulos has informed me that the widow of his latest victim has come to him to report a crime, the nature of which he had never previously conceived. It was all that Papadopoulos could do to prevent her from travelling to these shores in order to exact a terrible revenge upon the man responsible for her husband's death."

"Good heavens Holmes, I should wager that he was the man on the beach!" I exclaimed.

"I should be very much surprised if that were not the case and the Inspector has even gone on to identify him as a certain Sokratis Mavrapanos who just happens to hail from Athens. However, the remarkable thing is that his wife, Helena, is not even aware of her husband's tragic and untimely death!"

By this time my mind had been spinning itself into a maelstrom of confusion.

"I do not understand. Why should the dead man's wife be seeking revenge, whilst still believing her husband to be alive?"

"Ah, well now we come to the crux of the matter. According to Papadopoulos, Dragos does not actually kill his victims. Using his great and subtle skills, he will somehow induce his prey to digest the variety of poison that best suits his purpose at the time. However, the wonder of the thing is that he will then offer them the opportunity to counter the effects of the poison with a specifically prepared antidote. As you might have gathered, this great bounty comes at an enormous price and in many cases the victim has been rendered impoverished as a result.

"Sokratis Mavrapanos had been left a penniless and broken man and he came to London to seek the help of the only friend who he felt might have been able to help him. No doubt he regarded the acquisition of the treasure, or part of it, as his only route to financial reparation. The tragic result of this mission you have already been witness to, of course, but perhaps the motives of the man whom you have much maligned, may have improved your perception of Menachem Goldman?"

"My goodness Holmes," I said breathlessly. "Dragos' crime is nothing less than extortion by poison, or rather the threat of it. He has no real interest in the treasure at all! Obviously with the legendary universal antidote in his possession, he would regard his power as being almost infinite and absolute."

"Of course, that would be a most extreme and emotional point of view, although one that an egocentric like Dragos would be more than capable of. However, we must not lose sight of the fact that he would also regard the antidote as his line of final defence.

"Remember Watson that Sokratis Mavrapanos is only one of a countless number of poor souls, who have fallen prey to Dragos' repugnant schemes. The Count will only be too well aware that each one of his victims must henceforth be regarded as a potential and vengeful enemy. Therefore, the 'Mithradate' is Dragos' impenetrable shield against the sword of Damocles, which is forever hanging over his head," Holmes dramatically concluded.

"The whole thing is almost inconceivable," I gasped. "Although I will still need to be persuaded to your view that Goldman has no ulterior motive behind his consorting with his late friend. After all, there is still a valuable treasure to be considered, and Goldman probably saw the tragic Mavrapanos as a potential lead to a fortune," I added defiantly.

However, in that moment and seemingly oblivious to my last statement, Sherlock Holmes suddenly appeared to go into a deep state of shock. Throughout our entire association I had never before seen his complexion turn so pallid, nor witnessed his features contort with such anxiety. He strode over to the desk and began to write feverishly.

"I have been an abject and near-sighted fool, Watson, and my lack of hindsight has surely placed the lives of two men of our association in the greatest peril." He continued to write even while explaining to me the reason for his angst.

"I have perilously underestimated our adversary. Any man, who has been able to identify and locate so precious a commodity in such a far-off land and then make away with his greatest known threat, should have received a good deal more than my utmost consideration. The visit of our unannounced guests confirms that Count Dragos is obviously all too aware of our involvement in this matter. Therefore, as a result of such close surveillance, it must follow that the Count already knows of our connections to both Menachem Goldman and Denbigh Grey!

"My negligence might result in the gravest of consequences for both of them and I pray that these warnings are not already too late..........."

****

Chapter Eight: The Papers of Denbigh Grey

"Watson, I have to admit that in the calibre of criminal, with whom I have engaged throughout my career, I have indeed been most fortunate," Holmes stated, once he had been certain that the wires had been despatched with due alacrity.

"I find that to be a surprising, almost obscene turn of phrase in the context of the horrendous crimes that those individuals had perpetrated." I responded with not a little indignation.

"No, no, no Watson, you misunderstand me. I speak merely from a professional perspective without passing judgement on the immoral aspects of those criminals and their respective transgressions," Holmes hurriedly replied, while shaking his head slowly and repeatedly. "Consider, if you would, the notion of my being a maestro of the violin. Surely then, you would expect me to be more fulfilled in my performing the great works of Beethoven or Mozart, for example, as opposed to those of a nondescript scribbler of tunes?"

"I suppose so," I admitted reluctantly, although to me it still seemed to be a most cold-blooded way of seeing things.

I could see that Holmes had been warming to his subject, for he pulled his cherry wood pipe down from the mantelpiece, a sure sign that he was in a disputatious frame of mind. This surprised me somewhat under the rather fraught circumstances in which we found ourselves, although it did also occur to me that he had been attempting to divert his attention away from his understandable anxiety.

"Obviously the late mastermind, Professor Moriarty, will always predominate as the most illustrious of our previous protagonists. However, both Baron Gruner and that most contemptible master blackmailer, Charles Augustus Milverton, had also been at the very pinnacle of their respective fields. Therefore, it almost seems to be a form of poetic justice that we should now find ourselves confronted by the self-styled 'Poison King', does it not?" My friend's perverse reasoning caused a shiver to invade my spine.

I had been on the point of suggesting to Holmes that there was nothing remotely poetic about the terrible threat of life that was hanging over two of our associates, when I was spared any more of this most curious and disquieting dialogue by the sound of a summons at the street door.

A moment later, the door was pushed open to reveal a heavy set, middle-aged man who, for all the world, was every inch the epitome of an English country gentleman. The fellow had been bedecked in a very fine tan tweed suit, a pair of solid brown brogues and he had been brandishing a heavy and most threatening looking gnarled old wooden cane.

"Good afternoon gentlemen," he announced expansively. Holmes and I had both been taken aback by our guest's unmistakable accent, for surely, the man standing before us, was none other than Menachem Goldman!

"Good heavens Goldman!" I exclaimed. "The transformation is miraculous!"

For his part, Holmes leant forward in his chair and clapped his hands in a joyous round of applause.

"You may very well applaud me gentleman, but I can assure you that I have not taken on this persona with any great desire or pleasure. You should be in very little doubt that the disappearance of my friend had alerted me to the dangers that threaten me, long before I ever received your warning Mr. Holmes. Therefore, I have donned this disguise as a matter of dire necessity."

"Perhaps you should take a seat and a cup of tea," Holmes suggested, no doubt aware of the fact that Goldman was still ignorant of the fate of Mr. Mavrapanos.

After Holmes had called down for some tea, Goldman settled into a chair.

"Your arrival is most timely, for we had been growing increasingly concerned as to your well-being," I told him.

"No doubt, Dr. Watson, but believe me when I tell you that your concern was no greater than my own. However, I came to tell you that my sources have informed me of some disappointing news. Apart from the parchment that I passed over to you, only a tiny portion of the real treasure has found its way to these shores. The vast majority still remains in unknown hands, somewhere in Greece."

Just then Mrs. Hudson arrived with our tea and after Holmes had poured a cup out for our guest, Goldman gave voice to his concern.

"Mr. Holmes, I am most surprised and disappointed to see how indifferent you are to my latest information."

"By no means indifferent, Mister Goldman, but I have to tell you that certain recent events have led to the mere and avaricious quest for treasure paling into insignificance," Holmes replied.

"I am of little doubt that the parchment is at the core of your change of attention and priority," Goldman suggested glumly.

"Most certainly the parchment has assumed a far greater importance than even I could have envisioned. However, I have to inform you that the fate of a certain Greek gentleman of your acquaintance, Mister Sokratis Mavrapanos, has also come to our attention."

"You have been able to identify my friend?"

"Sadly, we were called upon by the Kentish police to assist in their investigations. No doubt fuelled by the same disappointing news that you have also received, it seems that Mister Mavrapanos had decided to return to Greece with all speed. Apparently he was set upon while on the train to Ramsgate, the ferry from there being the first stage of his journey home. As a result of this encounter, his lifeless body was subsequently discovered, apparently washed up on the beach of Westgate upon Sea, in Kent. However, it was the cause of his death that had alerted me to the threat to your life also. He had been poisoned."

93

Goldman had been visibly taken aback by this news and he sat in silence for a moment or two, while he digested the facts and their implications.

"It is an unusual cause of death to be sure, especially under that set of circumstances. However, I fail to see why you should feel that it increases the threat to my own life," Goldman stated with false nonchalance, although it was obvious to any observer that the significance of Holmes' news had not been lost on him.

"I will not burden you still further with the details, but I can assure you that the parchment is at the very core of your dilemma. We have all been watched most scrupulously, ever since the inception of the search for the treasure and I am in little doubt that anybody who has had a connection to that quest and my subsequent investigations has the same dark cloud hanging over them."

Goldman suddenly leapt up from his chair and glared down at my friend, obviously in a state of quite understandable terror.

"So, what am I to do, Mr. Holmes?" He pleaded desperately.

"To begin with, you must calm your nerves, Mister Goldman, for your situation may be not as bleak as first appears. There are three men involved, and for the moment their attentions have been drawn elsewhere. Do you, by any chance, have the means to undertake a journey to Greece?"

"I believe I do Mr. Holmes, but for the life of me I can think of no good reason for you to ask me such a thing."

"Mr. Goldman, I propose such a trip as I am of the opinion that a visit to the widow Mavrapanos might be in order at this time. I am sure that the poor woman would welcome your friendly and sympathetic support and perhaps an opportunity to locate the missing treasure might present itself to you while you are over there?"

Goldman returned to his seat and gave some serious consideration to Holmes' outlandish suggestion.

"There is very little doubt that such a journey will certainly keep me out of harm's way for a while. Besides which, there is reason to suppose that some good may come out of it, at the end of the day." Goldman's brave words belied the fact that there was a nervous tremor in his hand and a few beads of perspiration upon his knotted brow.

Nevertheless, my friend had evidently decided to ignore the fact that Goldman was still apprehensive of making such a journey.

"I shall give you the name and address of a friend of mine with the Athenian police force, who might be of material assistance to you, in your more lawful pursuits, of course." Holmes had emphasised the penultimate word of his last sentence, with a raised eyebrow and an ironic smile.

"You should not delay, however, for our enemies shall not be diverted for too much longer, I assure you."

Goldman received Holmes' note and his dire warning with a nervous smile and a garbled word or two of gratitude.

"No doubt you will keep us informed of the outcome of your journey." Holmes suggested before ushering Goldman towards the door and then closing it hurriedly upon our flustered guest.

An instant later Holmes was pulling on his coat and he instructed me to do likewise.

"Come Watson, we also have very little time to lose!"

I realised at once that Holmes' sudden burst of urgency had been galvanised by the fact that Goldman had responded to his wire and that Denbigh Grey had been disquietingly conspicuous by his absence and continued silence.

"No doubt you will be able to recollect Grey's address on this occasion?" Holmes' sarcasm had not been lost on me and I hurriedly pulled on my coat without honouring Holmes with a response.

Mercifully we had no great trouble in securing a cab for ourselves and I am certain that we had completed the two mile journey to Bloomsbury in a bone-shattering record time! Buoyed by our initial success, Holmes had seated himself on the edge of his seat, thereby ensuring that he had been poised to disembark immediately upon our arrival.

However, once we had turned the final corner, Holmes' enthusiasm soon waned, and the cause of my friend's deflation became instantly apparent. A police wagon had pulled up directly in front of Denbigh Grey's mansion building and there, standing right beside the vehicle, was our old friend from Scotland Yard, Inspector Lestrade!

Even though the once hostile and mistrustful relationship between the two men had mellowed somewhat in recent years, I could sense a great reluctance in my friend to face his old adversary on this occasion. Under the current set of circumstances, I found this to be entirely understandable, for there had been only one disquieting conclusion to be drawn from Lestrade's presence. Before stepping down from the cab, Holmes' steadied his nerves with a few deep breaths, but I could tell that he had been deeply affected by the dark inevitably of our tragic discovery.

Evidently Lestrade had been made aware of our presence within an instant of our arrival, and he buzzed over to our cab with a determined exigency.

"Mr. Holmes and Doctor Watson, I did not think that it would be too long before we saw you here! Normally your timely arrival might be put down to an uncanny coincidence; however, on this occasion I thought it to be almost inevitable. Now please, do not feign ignorance at this stage of the game." This last, ironic statement had, no doubt, been in response to the sombre and impassive manner with which Holmes had acknowledged the detective.

Holmes had stepped down from the cab slowly and deliberately and I could sense his reluctance to enter the building.

"Lestrade," Holmes doffed his hat as he joined him at the foot of the stairs that led to Denbigh Grey's mansion building.

There had been a cloud of dread and remorse, about my friend, that had not escaped the wily detective. Therefore, Lestrade greeted me with a questioning glance that I pretended to ignore.

"Your presence and that of the wagon seem to indicate a case of murder," I volunteered.

Lestrade nodded his affirmation.

"Indeed doctor and a most callous affair it is to boot. However, this awful crime could so easily have been averted....."

"How so?" Holmes suddenly blurted out.

"Oh, so we finally have your attention, Mr. Holmes." Lestrade responded sarcastically as he led us up the stairs. "Perhaps you would be good enough to share your knowledge of this sorry business before I offer you mine," Lestrade called over his shoulder while arriving on the second floor landing.

"I can assure you Inspector that I possessed no prior knowledge of this tragic business, although I did not consider it to be unlikely. Suffice it to say that Mr. Denbigh Grey had been undertaking a little historical research on my behalf, and his failure to contact me, within a reasonable period of time, had led me to become most anxious for his well-being."

"I would say that it would be considerably more than just 'a little historical research' for you to have become so concerned on his behalf," Lestrade astutely pointed out.

"There was the small matter of a valuable ancient treasure at the heart of this research, but the exact details of this had been secreted within a labyrinth of ancient Greek writing, a language of which Grey had been an uncommon master. Now I fear that those secrets might be lost forever." By the end of this sentence, Holmes' voice had begun to trail away into a barely discernible whisper.

"Hmm, well this still sounds like a lot of old poppycock to me! Lost treasures, ancient Greek writings and the like, I must say!" The ever-sceptical detective had been positively red faced with frustration and indignation, but before he could berate my friend still further, I reminded him of his previous statement.

"Inspector, you have yet to explain to us how this sorry business might have been averted."

Lestrade calmed himself with a few deep breaths before replying, although Holmes had already started to examine the carpeting immediately outside the apartment that I had just subtly indicated to him. All the while he had been listening attentively to Lestrade's explanation, although with no obvious indication that he had been doing so. Consequently, Lestrade had addressed himself to me exclusively, while I had taken out my notebook and pencil, with the Inspector's reluctant consent.

Just then we became aware of a nervous-looking, middle-aged gentleman who had been standing in a darkened corner of the landing. He had stepped forward into the light once he realised that Lestrade's attention was being drawn towards him. The man had been rubbing his forehead repeatedly and his peculiar looking tuffs of wispy white hair were constantly being moved back and forth by this nervous action. Despite the seasonal weather, he appeared to be perspiring rather profusely.

"You might be interested to know that this gentleman, Mr. Percy Linton, arrived at the door of Mr. Grey while the intruders were actually still inside! You see, it is customary for the two of them to meet here prior to attending a weekly game of whist at a small local club. Unusually and tragically, as it transpired, on this occasion Mister Linton arrived five minutes later than the appointed time." Lestrade explained.

Holmes finally jumped back onto his feet and turned to face the nervous whist player with an encouraging smile.

"Mr. Linton, could you kindly describe for me, as accurately as you are able, everything that you saw and heard upon your arrival?" Holmes suggested.

"I have it all here, Mr. Holmes," Lestrade confirmed, while offering Holmes the use of his notebook.

"Thank you Inspector Lestrade, but nevertheless I would far rather hear it from Mr. Linton's own lips, if neither of you object to that, of course." There had been something almost intimidating in Holmes' tone and both men immediately responded in the affirmative, and Lestrade formally introduced Holmes to Mr. Linton.

"As the Inspector correctly described, my usual routine at home had been somewhat disrupted this evening by the late return of my wife. She had been paying a visit to her ailing mother, and as a consequence, my supper had been slightly delayed, resulting in my tardy arrival here," Linton explained.

"That was most inconsiderate of your mother-in-law," I muttered while continuing to take notes. I noticed a wry smile of approval from my friend.

Linton cleared his throat and his face reddened still further.

"Well, that is as may be; however, I must confess that I was most surprised to find that Grey had not been waiting for me at the street door, for he has always been most meticulous with his time-keeping. Consequently, I rushed up the stairs to offer my apologies. I knocked sharply on his door, and I was then further taken aback by, what I thought at the time to be Grey's refusal to open it. I repeated my summons several times before I became aware of the sounds of commotion coming from the other side of his door."

"What exactly had been the nature of these sounds?" Holmes asked.

"They are rather difficult to describe exactly, for initially there had been nothing definitive or obvious.

Grey's voice had certainly sounded agitated and concerned, but I soon became aware of the sound of other voices, although I must confess that I could not make out a single word that was being said."

"Do you think this was due to the thickness of the door and their whispered tones, or could they perhaps have been speaking in a foreign tongue?" Holmes asked.

"Now that you happen to mention it, they might well have been speaking in a different language, but again I could not say that with any certainty. Nevertheless, by now I had become gravely concerned, and once I heard the unmistakable sound of a piece of furniture being overturned, I could not contain myself any longer!

"I increased the intensity of my blows upon the door and when I began to call out to my friend, it had been with such fervour that, before too long, other doors began to open along the landing, revealing several faces of concern from amongst Grey's neighbours."

"It had been at this point that the alarm had been raised and the police had been immediately summoned," Lestrade explained.

Holmes nodded his acknowledgement and encouraged Linton to conclude his account with an impatient movement of his hand.

"Suddenly and without a moment's notice, the door had been flung open and two large ruffians, dressed from head to toe in black, burst from Grey's room with such violence that I had been shoved against the opposite wall in their wake! The men disappeared down the stairs in an instant, and I took a few tentative steps through the doorway to my friend's room." Linton had clearly been greatly disturbed by the sight that greeted him and he paused breathlessly at his awful recollection.

"There is no real need for Mr. Linton to continue with his painful story, Mr. Holmes, for his discovery, once inside Grey's room, is only too clear for all to see," Lestrade suggested with a surprising display of compassion.

Holmes was in obvious agreement with the detective, for he dismissed Percy Linton with a single and condescending wave of his hand as he moved towards the door to Grey's room. Once inside we closed the door behind us and Holmes threw his coat down to the floor in an all too familiar dramatic fashion.

Lestrade had been correct in his assertion, for there was no doubting the chain of events that had taken place. In the centre of a small, beam-lined room, stood the chaotic desk of Denbigh Grey and across the desk was slumped the lifeless body of its tragic owner.

"I trust that nothing here has neither been moved nor altered?" Holmes asked anxiously.

"I assure you, Mr. Holmes, that all is exactly as we found it," Lestrade confirmed.

Holmes requested some room for his examination by rotating his long outstretched arms. He encouraged me to examine the body of the historian, while he threw himself down upon his stomach as he began to scrutinize every square inch of the large circular rug that sat beneath the desk. With his magnifying glass he then examined the door and desk in the most meticulous fashion. He seemed to attach great importance to the chaotic mound of papers that had saturated the surface of the dead man's desk, as he paid them particular attention.

Holmes and I reached our respective conclusions almost simultaneously and he recommended that Lestrade have the body removed without a moment's further delay. The detective hurried from the room, but once we heard him descending the stairs, Holmes began to move his fingers lightly and furtively amongst some of Grey's papers. I took up a position by the door to ensure that Holmes should not be interrupted, and by the time that Lestrade had returned with his men, a bundle of Grey's manuscripts had been safely deposited within Holmes' inside coat pocket. Leaving the constables to carry out their grim task, the three of us slowly descended the stairs towards the street below.

It took me no time at all to pass on my own findings, as Grey's death had undoubtedly been the result of a powerful blow to the back of head. I had noticed a sharp edged, glass paperweight that had been teetering on the edge of the desk and this had corresponded exactly to the size and shape of Grey's fatal wound.

Holmes looked at me thoughtfully while he lit a cigarette.

"So your conclusion would be that the attack had not been a premeditated affair?" Holmes asked.

"I regard it to be highly unlikely; after all, those villains had no idea that the paper weight would even have been there," I confirmed and Holmes accepted my conclusions with a nod of his head.

"Did your examination reveal anything of significance?" Lestrade had directed his inquiry to my friend.

Holmes slowly shook his head.

"I can only confirm the claims of Percy Lipton and the conclusions of the good doctor. Obviously the intruders had not come with the express purpose of killing Mr. Grey, but they decided that his death had become their only means of protecting their identities and intentions. The disorderly state of Grey's papers seems to indicate that they had been the intruders' principle objective. Sadly Mr. Grey has paid the ultimate price for his courage, for I am sure that his refusal to cooperate resulted in his violent death." Holmes appeared to be greatly saddened by this conclusion and he turned away from us both.

Lestrade viewed Holmes with more than a just little suspicion, and he rubbed the stubble on his chin while he formulated his next question.

"Hmmm, so you say, Mr. Holmes, however, I sense something in your manner that tells me that you know something more of these men than you are willing to divulge. I have warned you on many occasions of the consequences of withholding vital information from the official force!"

"Lestrade, I can assure you that I know little more than you do," Holmes replied with a winning smile. "Nevertheless, if you would indulge me for just forty eight hours, I will deliver to you, not only the identities of the two men who have been here today, but also the far more formidable mastermind who is behind everything that they do. If you stay alert for my summons and act upon it immediately, I will present you with a man who is sought after throughout the length and breadth of the entire continent!" Holmes pronounced dramatically.

"Well, I suppose that your methods have proved to be of some material assistance to Scotland Yard, from time to time." Lestrade failed to conceal a teasing smile.

"Hah! That is gracious of you to say so, Lestrade, but please stay alert, for when the time comes I assure you that we shall not have a moment to lose."

Holmes doffed his hat to the detective as we moved towards our cab and his smile, when he patted his pocket, told me that he had been more than satisfied with his ill-gotten bounty. Clearly Denbigh Grey had been successful in his endeavours, but sadly that noble historian had not lived long enough to be aware of the results.

Although it had not really surprised me; I was distressed to think that the poignancy of Grey's posthumous triumph had surely been lost on Sherlock Holmes. It then occurred to me that my friend's display of emotion, upon the discovery of Grey's demise, was probably born more of his injured ego and his failure to have protected him, than for the loss of the historian's life.

For now, however, my friend's remarkable mind was being directed towards other matters.

****

Chapter Nine: The Hostage

Upon our return to Baker Street, Holmes decided to waste very little time in making his intentions known to me.

I noted, with not a little dismay, that almost every piece of his vast array of laboratory equipment was about to be employed. Chemistry had always been a great passion of his; however, the intensity with which he was now going about his work showed me that he had no intention of engaging in any sort of recreational experiment.

My past experience impelled me to fling open each one of our windows and I took refuge in a corner of the room behind a barricade of the morning's newspapers. I braced myself for the avalanche of nauseous gasses and toxic smells, which had normally resulted from his experiments and before too long, my worst fears had been fully realised.

I knew that any protests on my part were destined to fall upon deaf ears. However, when I had been on the point of finally admitting defeat by retreating from the room, I noted with interest that my friend had taken out the papers that he had procured from the desk of Denbigh Grey. Holmes spread them out before him and he used them as a point of reference while he feverishly mixed his potions together.

I returned to my chair in the hope that Holmes might soon be able to divulge to me the nature of his discoveries. For the next hour or so, this eventuality became progressively less likely, for his work had been producing an endless cacophony of loud grunts and groans of disappointment followed by the abandonment of one experiment after another. His test tubes continued to emit all manner of noxious smoke and atmospheres, and his Bunsen burners had been continuously ablaze.

Finally, when I had incorrectly assumed that Holmes had reached the point of defeat and despair, he let out a victorious cry and clapped his hands together repeatedly in a dance of triumph. I was in little doubt that my inscrutable friend had no intention of divulging the nature of his discoveries to me, at this time. However, when he called me over to join him in a celebratory aperitif from the whiskey decanter, I accepted his invitation whole-heartedly.

"Might I further propose, friend Watson, that we sweep away these noxious odours and the traumatic events of the day, with a meal at Marcini's?" Holmes jovially suggested.

"I should be delighted!" I responded while getting down my coat.

While I waited for Holmes to set his toilet to rights, I was bound to consider the very real possibility that our current case might now be very close to a successful conclusion. Marcini's was a very fashionable eatery, in close proximity to Queen's Hall, and its elegant art nouveau frontage had welcomed many a venerated artist or musician through the years.

On the rare occasion that we had passed through its portal, it had been at the very conclusion to a challenging case. Therefore, as our meal progressed towards its delicious conclusion, I had been expecting my friend to elaborate upon the meaning behind the apparent success of his experiments. However, I was soon to discover that nothing could have been further from Holmes' mind.

As each course had come and gone, I found my friend to be at his most stimulating and eloquent, and he had waxed lyrical upon subjects as diverse as the merits and breathing techniques of the pre-eminent tenor of the day, de Reszkes and even Holmes' own and extensive research into the life and times of Mithradates VI himself!

I must confess that by the time that the bill had been paid and we had ventured outside once more to secure the services of a cab, all thoughts of Count Dragos and his dark and manipulative plans had been dispelled by the delightful and informative dissertations of my friend, Sherlock Holmes.

However, that state of affairs did not last for very long, for Holmes soon informed me that his research had also extended to the current King of Poisons as well as that of the ancient warrior.

"I do hope that your discoveries will prove to be of some material assistance in bringing the man to justice." I said, while I sat back in anticipation.

"Unfortunately my discoveries are not really pertinent to our current dilemma, although I have found, on more than one occasion that a certain knowledge of a man's background and motivations can often prove to be an aid in predicting the mechanics of his mind and therefore his subsequent actions. Consider this, if you will. Our friend, Count Dragos, grew up within a very privileged set of circumstances. His family estate had been a grand one indeed, and Dragos received not only each and every one of his heart's desires, but also a home education of the very highest standard. Therefore, the extent of his intellect and the range of his knowledge cannot be held in doubt. Sadly for him, this Utopian existence did not last long and after the tragic loss of his mother to tuberculosis when he was only seven years of age, the young boy retreated into a very dark and solitary place. According to all accounts, his father had never been of an affectionate or paternal nature, and after the death of his wife; he became even more neglectful of his son.

Consequently the boy's upbringing comprised only of the pandering of his many servants and the dry, dusty books of the elderly scholars who had been sent to tutor him. Ancient history and the classics soon proved to be his most favoured subjects, and as he grew older he gradually developed a fascination upon the history of King Mithradates Vl." My friend paused to light a cigarette, and he smiled when he noticed how enthralled I had been by his discourse.

"My, my, to think that so toxic an obsession should have begun at so young an age," I mentioned while sadly shaking my head.

"Yes indeed Watson, but as we now know that keen interest of his did not end there. According to some of the servants, as the young lad grew towards adolescence a sinister, almost malevolent side to his nature began to manifest itself. He expressed a great interest in the universal antidote, and the servants often recoiled in horror when they observed the callous manner in which he experimented upon various small animals, with his battery of toxins and antitoxins.

Even the family pet, a particularly affectionate Golden Labrador called Max, had not been immune to his dark researches. There had actually been a rumour that a retired servant, who had been bequeathed a small cottage on the boundaries of the estate in which to see out his twilight years, had met with an unusual and untimely death! Apparently, the old man's body had been found covered in unsightly red blemishes, but the family doctor, who had hurriedly confirmed a death by natural causes, disappeared without trace shortly after those events took place."

"Good heaven's Holmes, surely a further examination must have taken place?" I gasped.

Holmes gravely shook his head.

"Apparently not Watson, however a few years later an event occurred that would alter the shape of the young man's destiny forever. When Dragos' father finally capitulated to a long-standing and chronic heart condition, it was naturally assumed that the young Count would come into a considerable inheritance. However, his lawyers soon discovered that his father had not only squandered a vast fortune on mere trifles and indulgences, but his mismanagement had left the entire estate in financial ruin.

"Within a short while each one of his late father's associates and advisors began to distance themselves from the whole sorry mess, and at the age of just twenty-two years, the young Count Dragos found himself to be homeless, destitute and quite alone," Holmes concluded.

"My goodness, it does not need a huge stretch of the imagination to infer that Dragos then decided to make his own way in the world, by putting to use the only skill that his privileged upbringing had ever allowed him to acquire."

"Exactly, Watson! Obviously, his inherently malevolent nature also meant that the transition to such a way of life would have been far easier for him than for most. It is impossible to condone his vile actions by reason of his tragic early life, but it is now far easier for us to understand the source of his ruthlessness and his total disregard for any form of life. Watson, we must guard against this fiend with such vigilance as we have never employed before!"

By this time we had found ourselves back in Baker Street. The dark grey mist of a chill autumn night had gradually descended and the light, rasping wind had caused the murky vapour to swirl rhythmically around the flickering gas lamps. We dismissed the cab, but as I began to ascend the steps and ready my key, Holmes suddenly restrained me from my actions with a talon like grip upon my wrist.

"Something is not right here, Watson. See, there is not a single light on in the place, and Mrs Hudson always leaves at least one lamp alight when we are expected home at so late an hour," Holmes whispered hoarsely while crouching down to examine the damp step beneath his shoes.

He remained thus for what seemed to be an eternity; although in reality it had only been for a minute or two. However, when he finally straightened himself once more, there was an aura of gravity upon his features that immediately filled me with a terrible sense of dread.

"Two very familiar sets of boot prints have ascended the steps, although I can detect only one set leading away from here....and there is one other scuff mark." Holmes' voice was now barely audible, but I had heard enough to convince myself that leaving my revolver in the drawer upstairs had proved to have been a grave error indeed!

My sense of foreboding was heightened, still further, by the sight of Holmes reversing his cane and then testing the weight of its loaded handle, by slapping it repeatedly into the palm of his hand. All the while, the thought of Mrs. Hudson's potential fate tested my nerves to their very limits.

Holmes raised his cane, as if poised to carry out a strike and I followed closely behind him as we slowly ascended the seventeen steps that led to the first floor landing. Our experience of each and every irregularity, that had infiltrated that ancient staircase, had enabled us to complete the climb without having caused even the slightest of sounds, and we arrived at the door to our rooms in a state of breathless expectancy and anxiety.

Holmes gestured for me to retrieve my revolver from the floor above and I did so without a moment's hesitation. With that cold and steely comfort held securely within my grasp, I rejoined my friend as he was about to wrap his hand around the door handle. All the while, there had been neither sight nor sound of our landlady, and I clenched the handle of my revolver with a determined resolve.

Without a moment's warning, Holmes swiftly turned the handle and he slammed the door open with enough force to cause it to rebound off of the adjacent wall! The two of us readied our weapons and immediately confronted the tall and darkened shape that had occupied a space in front of the large bay window.

Holmes' examination of the front steps had revealed an accurate conclusion, for there had only been one person present to occupy our attention. While I held my revolver trained upon the intruder, Holmes turned on the oil lamp closest to him. The weak, orange glow revealed one of the men who had previously paid us an unsolicited call and it was neither possible nor indeed necessary for us to be able to differentiate the one from the other.

Suffice it to say, that Holmes and I had only one question for this blackguard, but the man volunteered an explanation before either of us had a chance to ask for one. It had been obvious from his posture and demeanour that he had no violent or threatening intent towards us, so Holmes slowly lowered his cane. For my part, however, I had no intention of doing likewise with my gun!

"Gentlemen, neither of you have anything to fear from me, I assure you. Your landlady is quite safe," The man said, as he glanced anxiously towards my revolver.

I levelled the barrel at the man's head, by way of a response. He greeted my gesture with a short wry laugh and then moved towards the centre of the room to where he could be seen more clearly.

"Stay right where you are," I warned the bounder.

There had been something strangely ominous about the sight of the large, darkened form of the man as he emerged from the shadows and then seeing him being doused in the dim ochre glow of a single oil lamp. Nevertheless, I kept my nerve and neither my eyes nor the barrel of my gun left him for an instant. Once again he had bared his blackened teeth, as if he had still been in control of the situation.

"Where is Mrs. Hudson?" I barked and Holmes placed a calming hand upon my arm.

"Obviously we arrived this evening in full expectation of your having fulfilled your side of the bargain. However, in your absence my colleague and I decided to take out a little insurance policy, just to confirm to you the gravity of your situation. Mrs. Hudson, as you call her, is temporarily residing aboard a small houseboat, which is moored in the area known by you Londoners as Little Venice. There she will remain, until such time as you arrive with her ransom."

"No doubt you are referring to the Mithradate, otherwise known as the 'universal antidote'. Unless I am very much mistaken, the remainder of Lucullus' lost treasure is of little or no importance either to you or to your employer," Holmes speculated with surprising calm.

"Naturally you are quite correct; Mr. Holmes and we would have expected nothing less from you. As you are doubtless aware, our employer has a particular and personal interest in the antidote, one that perhaps even you may not fully comprehend."

Despite the presence of my weapon, the man began to move towards the door and I crossed over to bar his way. The man slowly shook his head condescendingly.

"Oh Doctor Watson, I can assure you that should I not return to the houseboat by a given time, my colleagues will not hesitate for a moment in taking the life of your landlady. For now she is quite comfortable and in good health, but that could change within an instant!"

The man placed a small buff envelope into the hands of my friend, which contained the full address of the houseboat and a description of the vessel.

"We have chosen this most singular location with good reason. I would strongly recommend that you two gentlemen bring no one else, for it is absolutely impossible to approach us without your being observed and recognised. However, should you decide to be so foolhardy, well......." He pointed at my gun and then, with a most sinister smile, the scoundrel emitted a vocal impression of the sound of gunshot.

"Do not disappoint us, Mr. Holmes, I beseech you. We shall expect you at the houseboat tomorrow evening at precisely six o'clock, with the Mithradate, of course." With that and a final smirk at me and my gun, the man was gone.

For a moment Holmes and I just stood there, neither of us being capable of either speech or movement.

Finally, my anxiety for the well-being of Mrs. Hudson and my frustration at having to let one of her captors walk away from us unhindered, spilled over into a vitriolic and irrational tirade against my friend.

"Upon my word Holmes, I simply cannot comprehend how you could possibly have played so loose with the life of Mrs. Hudson! You simply allowed one of her captors to walk away from here without a care in the world and you have condemned her to an unknown fate at their hands. After all, we do not even have the treasure with which to bargain, assuming, of course, that they intend to honour their part of the agreement at all! How could you do it?" I hurled my gun down on to one of the chairs and then stormed over to the far side of the room where I lit a cigarette.

I noticed my friend studying me with thoughtful and silent reflection, until the moment when he considered that the smoke and nicotine had had their calming effect. As it transpired, that moment would prove to be quite some time in coming. However, once Holmes could finally sense the mellowing of my mood, he was quick to put my mind at ease.

"Really Watson, I am most surprised to note that you are still ignoring my maxim regarding the dangers of making assumptions. As you will now see, it is detrimental to the process of logical thought and deduction and will lead you upon a long and difficult path away from the truth."

With a broad and dramatic sweep of his arm and a piercing laugh of triumph, Holmes produced Denbigh Grey's papers from within his inside pocket.

"Here, friend Watson, are our bargaining tools, the only treasure of King Mithradates that Count Dragos truly seeks!"

"The universal antidote!" I exclaimed.

"Exactly and as you will no doubt soon realise in the cold light of day, we had no other option but to allow that fellow to return to his lair. By what other means were we to guarantee the well-being of Mrs. Hudson? Now, however, it is our turn to take out an insurance policy."

With that, Holmes turned to his desk and began to hurriedly compose a wire. With a poignancy, that had not even been lost upon my friend, it fell to me to ensure the wire's safe and urgent despatch, but I stopped in my tracks once I saw the name of the addressee, for it was none other than Inspector Lestrade!

"Oh come along, Holmes, you really cannot expect me to send this?" I protested. "Surely, in the light of Dragos' reputation for ruthlessness, his dire words of caution should not be taken so lightly."

"You must not despair, Watson, for I have plans for the good Inspector that will not jeopardise the well-being of Mrs. Hudson in any way, I assure you. However, you must not delay, for I have other preparations still to put in hand." Holmes suddenly disappeared into his room and as I set off on my mission, a discord of chaotic noises could be heard from behind my friend's door.

Naturally, I made good speed there and back, but I had arrived with barely enough time in which to see the results of Holmes boisterous and ear-splitting arrangements. Before me stood a bucolic, ancient sea dog, replete right down to an ominous facial scar and a wispy white moustache, a disguise which Holmes had employed on a few previous occasions. To add further to my confusion, Holmes was clasping in his right hand, what appeared to have been his overnight bag.

I had not the time to inquire as to the bag's purpose, for without another word, my friend was through the door and bounding down the stairs towards the street below.

Once again, I realised, that yet another long and frustrating vigil lay ahead for me, and I grudgingly picked up my latest reading material which I took over to the dying glow of our fire.

****

Chapter Ten: Count Dragos

The book had only sustained my interest for a short while and before too long I found my mind wandering back to the true purpose behind Holmes' disguise and his sudden departure with his bag in hand.

I came to the incontrovertible conclusion that Holmes had every intention of penetrating our enemy's territory, whilst remaining incognito. Obviously some knowledge of the lay of the land could prove to be invaluable in the process of weighing our options, although I could still not conceive of a reason behind the involvement of Inspector Lestrade nor the importance that Holmes had attached to his bag.

Surely my friend would not endanger the life of our landlady by flagrantly disregarding the very clear and stark warning of her captors? Suddenly my attention was drawn away from my fruitless speculations and towards a plain buff envelope that had been laying upon the dining table and which had, somehow, remained unnoticed. I tore the envelope open with great enthusiasm for I had immediately recognised the hand that had written the address.

The letter had been from none other than my beloved Sophie and to my mind, it had been long overdue in coming. To my immense joy, her business in Frinton had at last been concluded and she intended to return to London in two days' time, accompanied by her charming brother, Simon. However, my relief soon turned to anxiety when I considered the fact that the fate of Mrs. Hudson and the conclusion of the Count Dragos affair, might still be hanging in the balance by the time of my wife's return.

Sophie had already endured much throughout our relatively brief time together, but I felt confident in the certain knowledge that she would be tolerant of my absence under the extreme circumstances of our latest dilemma. Perhaps Holmes' reconnoitre would expedite an immediate culmination. In any event, I had no intention of abandoning my friend, or of turning away from the plight of Mrs. Hudson.

As it transpired, my fretfulness had very little time in which to intensify, for a few moments later came the unmistakable sound of the street door opening and closing. With a brief smile, I folded away Sophie's letter and put it into my pocket as I rose to greet my friend.

I was more surprised at the promptness of Holmes' return than I had been by the fact that he was not alone! Nevertheless, the sight of two ancient sea dogs standing before me had evidently produced a look of astonishment upon my face, which they had both found to be most amusing. Their laughter gradually subsided enough for them to be able to remove their disguises and I poured them each a warming glass of cognac.

To my amazement the other seaman had been Inspector Lestrade and the other little mystery had also been solved once he began to pack away his disguise into Holmes' overnight bag. The rather flushed detective swallowed his drink with great relish, for his camouflage had been a heavy one and his mission had been fraught with danger and mystery.

"Oh, Watson, I am much relieved to observe that you have found Lestrade's appearance to be so inscrutable. As you are doubtless aware, had we been observed as our usual selves, the life of our landlady would not have been worth a moment's purchase!" Holmes declared flamboyantly, before draining his glass.

"I have been more than just aware of that, I can assure you. As you know, I was somewhat appalled by the rather cavalier fashion in which you approached the very real threat that still hangs over the poor woman. Of course I am relieved that you both managed to remain undetected, but you must tell me now what information you managed to glean from your mission," I demanded excitedly.

"I take it that you are aware of the lateness of the hour?" Holmes asked mischievously.

"I shall not even consider retiring for the night until you have told me of your adventures and your findings!" I stated while returning resolutely to my chair.

At this juncture, Lestrade snatched up Holmes' bag and promised he would be at his assigned position at the time arranged for the following evening. With a grateful smile, Holmes led the Inspector to the door. Once he had been satisfied that the street door had been securely closed, my friend filled his old clay pipe, before joining me in the chair opposite to my own.

By now the fire had reached its chill nadir, and Holmes hurried to his room to fetch his purple dressing gown, which he then draped over his thin shoulders.

Holmes immediately recognised the fact that I was about to bombard him with a myriad of questions. My friend averted that situation with a dramatic wave of his arms and the promise of a full account of all that had transpired earlier. I could tell that it had gone well, for even through a thick plume of smoke, Holmes' triumphal smile shone through.

"I can assure you Watson, that had Lestrade and I arrived but a moment later than we had, the situation would have become an impossible one. We had little difficulty in identifying the houseboat in question, for the description with which we had been furnished, had been a detailed and accurate one and the adornment of the boat is most distinctive.

However, the location for a suitable place of our concealment took us a while longer to find. Then, with barely a moment to spare, just fifty yards away from Dragos' floating lair; we found a derelict old barge which had evidently been deserted and moored there for some considerable time. We took a position behind this sorry vessel and realised that this precise spot also afforded us with a decent enough vantage point for discreet observation.

Almost at once, we could hear two sets of footsteps walking purposefully towards us along the jetty. I do not mind telling you, Watson, that despite my confidence in our camouflage, I lost no time in hurling Lestrade down to the ground behind the barge, while I stole a brief glance before joining him there.

As you can imagine, I was able to recognise one of Dragos' henchmen almost at once, while beside him strode a most striking and singular looking individual. I was in no doubt that this was none other than the odious Count himself! Despite the repulsive nature of the trade that he plies, I can tell you that, in Count Dragos, we have been presented with a most impressive and formidable looking opponent.

He stands at the same height as his impressive subordinates, if not a fraction taller and his broad expanse of shoulders stretched his finely tailored overcoat almost to the breaking point. He too dresses exclusively in black and his immaculate beard and moustache are perfectly groomed and waxed. He sported an oversized monocle over his left eye, below which sits a large and ominous old scar."

"It is hard for me to comprehend how you managed to obtain so much information from so brief a study." I exclaimed, although I was now convinced that I too would now be able to identify the Count at a single glance, thanks to Holmes' descriptive attention to detail.

"The trained observer can glean more in the briefest instant, than an unaware person is able to after an hour's worth of hard study. Nevertheless, I must admit to being aided by the man's most individual features. I was much relieved to note that neither of them afforded our position even the briefest of glances and before long they had both boarded their boat and disappeared down below."

I shook my head in disbelief.

"My, my, that was indeed a close call." I admitted. "However, I must admit to remaining uneasy about the deployment of Inspector Lestrade, even if he was cloaked in so effective a disguise."

"Watson, what other choice do we have? Dragos and his men will expect nothing less than to see the two of us in our usual dress and persona. You can be assured that I shall not hesitate, even for a moment, in handing over that which Dragos so keenly seeks. However, once Mrs. Hudson is safely off the boat, I have no intention of allowing Dragos and his men to escape scot free!

"I promise you Watson, that once Mrs. Hudson is out of harm's way, Lestrade and his whistle will prove to be invaluable to us. He has been left in no doubt as to the consequences of his being recognised, but once assured of Mrs. Hudson's safety, Lestrade and his men, will secure the perimeter in an instant.

Oh Watson, it is a perilous undertaking that we are set upon, so please ensure that you have taken every precaution prior to our departure. Any deviation from our plans would have the gravest of results," Holmes warned me with unnecessary earnest.

"Holmes, you can be assured that my revolver and I shall be by your side, from the first to last!" I replied determinedly.

"I would expect nothing less of you, old fellow." Holmes smiled, although I thought that I could detect a concealed uneasiness in his manner.

"Holmes, do you suspect further treachery, even once the exchange has been concluded?" I asked with apprehension.

"I would certainly regard it as a distinct possibility." Holmes admitted in a tone that implied a sense of guilt. "There is much more to Dragos' ruthlessness than his desire to acquire the universal antidote." Holmes lapsed into a protracted and contemplative silence before continuing. "I am afraid that I have not been entirely candid with you, old friend."

An involuntary shudder came over me, "What do you mean Holmes?" I whispered hoarsely.

"I have led you to believe that Dragos' use of poison has been nothing more than a method of extorting money from his exalted victims. While this undoubtedly is true, I have failed to explain to you one of the reasons behind the Count's continued and relentless success. Inspector Papadopoulos has also included, in his recent correspondence to me, the speculative details of a more sinister and deadlier aspect to Dragos' crimes. Although it has yet to be proven in a court of law, my Greek colleague is convinced that Dragos increases the potency of his threats to one victim, by making an example of another. I am sure that it is now obvious to you that he employs the deadliest of means in achieving this."

"Good heavens Holmes, this blackguard will stop at nothing! However, I must say that I am a little surprised and disappointed by your decision to have withheld this information from me until now. After all, we have come up against a ruthless and murderous adversary on more than one occasion in the past, have we not?" I protested.

"Of course we have Watson, but I was afraid that your quite understandable concern for Mrs. Hudson might have compelled you to an uncharacteristic act of reckless and perilous indiscretion," Holmes admitted.

"Surely you share my concerns for her safety?" I asked with not a little disquiet.

"Indeed I do Watson, but your emotions run far deeper than my own. To me, every aspect of a case is just another factor, a problem to be overcome in my relentless pursuit of justice and the truth. I have to admit that you temper my cold analytical method with your kindlier nature and humanity."

Initially I could not be certain as to whether I had just been insulted or complimented by my friend. To Holmes, any display of emotion was seen as being a divergence, even a weakness, which was detrimental to the logical thought processes that were so vital to his profession. On the other hand, he had also just admitted that occasionally he needed to be reminded of the more human aspect of his unique vocation, a quality which I had been able to provide him with.

After further consideration, I finally arrived at the conclusion that neither an insult nor compliment had been intended. To the mind of Sherlock Holmes, such judgments didn't even exist, for they were both a departure from the path towards logic and absolute truth.

"I quite understand your reasoning, but you should not forget that I have seen active service during many a violent encounter and that I recognise, only too well, the dangers of thoughtless actions taken in the heat of the moment. When the time finally arrives, you may safely rely on that," I reminded him.

"Thank you Watson, but now might I suggest that we take to our beds. Before the day is out tomorrow, we shall require as much strength and energy as we can muster." Then to calm my nerves, Holmes produced the Mithradate once more and he waved the means of securing Mrs. Hudson's release, triumphantly above his head.

"Good night old fellow." I smiled, as I slowly made my way up the stairs.

I received no reply and I was certain that, for my friend, a long and lonely night with his pipe lay ahead.

****

Chapter Eleven: The Treasure of the Poison King

The following day passed very slowly indeed and the nervous tension, which had been steadily increasing as morning slowly turned to afternoon, had only been tempered for me by the thought of my beloved Sophie waiting for my return to our marital home.

Her brother, Simon, who had journeyed back with her from Frinton-On-Sea, had kindly offered to remain with her until such time as they had both been assured of the successful outcome of our undertaking. I felt grateful for this, even though Sophie still remained blissfully ignorant of the perilous nature of the coming evening's endeavour.

Holmes spent much of the day cross legged upon his chair in a state of deep meditation. This may sound surprising, in the light of Holmes' infamous lack of patience, but his plans had all been put in hand and each potential outcome had been allowed for in meticulous detail. He paid me little or no heed throughout much of the day, but on occasion I observed a fleeting and enigmatic smile play along his lips, which I felt had boded ill for those he sought to bring to justice.

The sight of this had imbued me with renewed optimism and confidence and after a light lunch, I returned to the task of cleaning my revolver whilst ensuring that each chamber had been fully loaded. Both Holmes and I then paid fastidious attention to our toilet and attire and therefore, by the time that the appointed hour had finally arrived, we had both considered ourselves to be as prepared as it was possible to have been.

Exactly on cue, we could hear our stalwart ally, Dave "Gunner" King; bring his cab up outside 221b. We made our leisurely way down the stairs and in a deliberately calm manner, Holmes and I climbed slowly aboard. My friend immediately instructed King to proceed to Little Venice at a more sedate speed than the one that he commonly employed when in our service. Apart from having been London's most knowledgeable and adroit cabbie, King's military experience had also made him invaluable to us both on those occasions when we had found ourselves in a particularly tight corner.

King merely shrugged his shoulders and unquestioningly did Holmes' bidding, ensuring that we barely broke from a walk throughout the entire, uneventful journey. Upon our arrival at the jetty of Little Venice, Holmes had been meticulous in positioning King and his faithful steed. He had to make sure that neither could be seen nor heard from Dragos' houseboat, while at the same time making certain that King would be able to hear our signal immediately and then act upon it in an instant.

Further along the road I could see parked up, a still and silent police vehicle, its occupants only at the beginning of a long and uncomfortable vigil. Only then, once Holmes had checked his pocket watch for the final time, did he feel confident enough in our punctuality to allow himself one final cigarette. I must say that I joined him in this with great enthusiasm and once we had concluded our smokes, we climbed down the steps towards the jetty.

Holmes had no real need to point out the boat in question, for its striking colours of orange and bright green had been as distinctive as he had previously described. Holmes motioned me to silence as we approached a derelict old barge and a moment later the reason for his caution became self-evident. I recognised at once the crouched figure behind the barge, for it had been none other than Inspector Lestrade, who, once again, had been fully bedecked in Holmes' iconic old sea dog disguise.

That trusty servant of Scotland Yard raised his hand briefly by way of acknowledging our arrival and Holmes tipped the front of his hat in reciprocation. We paused briefly, while Holmes confirmed the lay of the land for one final time and I then realised what a dark and chilly evening it had suddenly become. A light mist had descended upon the narrow waterway and the vaporous silence had been barely broken by the gentle lapping of the canal waters against the sides of the various barges and houseboats that had been moored there.

This time it was I who had checked the time and at precisely one minute before the hour of six o'clock, Holmes and I slowly descended the aged wooden steps that led us towards Mrs. Hudson's floating prison. For reassurance, I patted the revolver in my pocket for what had undoubtedly been the umpteenth time and I noticed Holmes conducting a similar exercise with Mrs. Hudson's ransom.

Despite our best efforts, it had proved to be impossible for us to have made a silent and undetected descent and before we even had a chance to knock upon the door; it had suddenly been flung open by Dragos' henchmen! I was dismayed by the thought of anything else that they might have observed during our long and deliberate approach. However, there had been something in their manner that convinced me that my fears had been unwarranted and they stood back to allow us to pass through the boat's low and narrow entrance.

I admit to having been oblivious to the presence of Count Dragos, so dismayed had I been at the sight of our landlady, who had been trussed up with some stout rope and within the confines of a tiny and uncomfortable looking wicker chair. She had clearly rested from her struggles a while ago and her relieved smile, upon witnessing our arrival, had been hopeful but very weary.

I only became aware of the Count, when he slowly unravelled his long frame from a chair that had been uncomfortably close to that of Mrs. Hudson. There had been nothing surprising to me in Dragos' appearance, so accurate had been Holmes' description of him, but his malevolent and triumphal smile had provoked a vengeful and violent intent within me, which I had not thought myself capable of previously.

Count Dragos walked slowly towards my friend and he appraised Holmes in a most disdainful and provocative manner. I had been greatly surprised by the calm and stoic way with which Holmes had reacted to Dragos' chiding.

"Well, well, I confess to being a little surprised and disappointed at the ease with which I have been able to overcome the illustrious Mr. Sherlock Holmes. It is hard for me to countenance that the master of logic and a man supposedly so bereft of any form of human emotion, could have been coerced into exchanging something as valuable as the 'Mithradate', for nothing more than the life of a mere landlady!

"Oh yes Doctor Watson, I have long been an avid reader of your romanticised accounts of Mr. Holmes' adventures and therefore, I am only too well aware of your venerated opinion of the man. Perhaps those evaluations of yours are somewhat wide of the mark and exaggerated?" Dragos suggested sarcastically.

I was in little doubt that Holmes could sense the rage that had been building up within me. He gripped my gun arm with a fierce and restraining force and he shook his head emphatically.

"That is a very wise decision, Mr. Holmes and perhaps, as a precaution against your impulsive tendencies, you would now be good enough to place your army revolver over here, Doctor Watson." Dragos tapped the surface of a small wooden table that had been positioned in the centre of the room.

It was with great reluctance that I relinquished my weapon and once he had been satisfied that Holmes and I were no longer a potential threat to him, the Count visibly relaxed. He removed his monocle, thereby revealing the true extent of the appalling scar beneath it. This ancient and probably well-deserved wound, contributed still further to his already imposing aura of menace. He clasped his hands together and then proceeded to crack his knuckles back and forth in a most nauseating manner.

"Mister Holmes, I suggest that we now get down to the business at hand. May I safely assume that you have brought the Mithradate with you and that it is on your person?" Dragos held out his hand in expectant receipt of the said manuscript, but he was sorely disappointed and not a little surprised, once he had realised that my friend had absolutely no intention of handing over the universal antidote, just yet.

"In keeping with the business-like manner of our transaction, I would prefer it if you first untie Mrs. Hudson and allow the good doctor here the opportunity to examine her and confirm her well-being," Holmes suggested impassively. All the while, his right hand remained inside his jacket, which indicated the location of the 'Mithradate'.

Dragos responded with a sardonic laugh.

"Mister Holmes, you are hardly in a position that would allow you the luxury of dictating the conditions of our exchange." Dragos indicated the two men who were stood to attention on either side of us.

"On the contrary, Mister Dragos, for I can assure you that I shall not hesitate for an instant, in destroying the manuscript before allowing it to fall into your hands, regardless of the consequences!" Holmes boldly declared.

Holmes removed his hands from his inside pocket and revealed, not the Mithradate, which we had all expected to see, but a Vesta match ready to be struck.

Reluctantly, Dragos instructed one of his men to do Holmes' bidding and I immediately stepped forward to examine the poor woman.

Mrs. Hudson had been shuddering from head to foot, out of sheer exhaustion as much as fear. Obviously, her wrists had been left chaffed and sore by the harshness of her bonds and when she had finally struggled to her feet; I could feel that her legs were weak and unsteady. Nevertheless, in all other respects she appeared to have remained in good general health and she bore no other signs of mistreatment or of malnutrition.

I indicated my satisfaction to Holmes, but instead of returning the match to its pocket and while still retaining possession of the manuscript, my friend set out one further condition to our captors.

"If you would now allow Doctor Watson to escort Mrs. Hudson into the reviving evening air, I am certain that you and I can conclude our business in a calm and amicable fashion. After all, Dr. Watson and I can no longer be regarded as a threat to you and should you feel that you need any further convincing, you can surely examine me for weapons," Holmes suggested, while raising his hands compliantly above his head.

Once again, Dragos nodded his agreement.

"That will not be necessary. Mr. Holmes, but one of my men will go with them, just to ensure that you have no further tricks up your sleeves. Perhaps then we may be able to bring matters to a speedy conclusion."

Dragos' man led the way up the stairs to the jetty and I supported Mrs. Hudson every step of the way, as she gingerly climbed her way to freedom.

The following events occurred with such rapidity, that it had been impossible for me to collate my thoughts until I finally came to record them for posterity. As soon as we three appeared upon the jetty, Holmes' plans were immediately set into motion.

We walked slowly past the dilapidated barge and Inspector Lestrade emerged stealthily from his hiding place, still in the guise of the old sea dog. With his revolver cocked and ready to fire, the Inspector strode towards Dragos' henchman and pressed the nozzle of his gun against the man's temple. No word of warning had been necessary and the man raised his hands above his head in resignation and surrender. Lestrade wasted no time at all in slapping a set of handcuffs upon the man's wrists and he dragged him off towards the wagon.

Simultaneously, Dave "Gunner" King drove his cab full pelt to where we had all been standing and I immediately bundled Mrs. Hudson, rather unceremoniously, into the back of the carriage. King cracked his whip, and I watched with much relief as our staunch ally conveyed our bewildered landlady out of harm's way and with all speed.

My thoughts and attention once more returned to the plight of my friend and I turned and raced back towards the houseboat. Without the comfort of my revolver, my plans had been unclear, but I had been determined to help Holmes in any way that I might. To my dismay, Dragos had anticipated my speedy return and his henchman immediately put his gun to my head as I climbed back aboard.

Once again, Dragos sniggered to himself and he held out his hand once more, to receive the universal antidote.

"Really gentlemen, this entire process has been so much easier than even I could have anticipated, or hoped for. Now please Mr. Holmes, do not stretch my tolerance any further. I would strongly suggest that you hand over the 'Mithradate', preferably before my colleague feels compelled to blow off the head of your good friend, Dr. Watson."

My heart was pounding as I watched Holmes place the parchment into Dragos' eager hand without a moment's hesitation. To my immense relief, Dragos henchman lowered the gun. However, the shrill sound of Lestrade blowing his whistle in the distance, as he summoned his constables to our aid, changed the dynamics of the situation once again.

Dragos' assured and arrogant manner altered dramatically, and as he slid the Mithradate into his inside pocket, we could see that he had recognised the perilous nature of his predicament. He snapped an order to his man that neither Holmes nor I should be allowed to move while he made his escape. The man pulled back the trigger of his gun, thereby leaving us in little doubt of his intention to use it, should he be so compelled. We had no choice, but to stand aside while Count Dragos made his way towards the door.

"It has indeed been a pleasure to have made your acquaintance, Mr. Holmes. Perhaps, after all, your reputation may not be mere hyperbole. Although, of course,

I will still achieve the object of my quest, whereas you will merely be returning home with nothing more than an aged servant. However, as they say, 'he who fights and runs away....'" Dragos had clearly decided that discretion would indeed be the better part of valour and we could soon hear his footsteps in the distance as he made good his escape.

A short while afterwards we could hear another set of footsteps, only this time they had been running in our direction and at a greater speed. Clearly, Lestrade had managed to secure Dragos' man aboard the police wagon and he was now returning to come to our aid. Although it was now too late for Lestrade to thwart Dragos' escape, the momentary distraction of his urgent approach caused our guard to look away for the briefest of instants.

It had been all the time that Holmes had needed and with a single movement he had grasped the man's wrist in his vice-like grip. The ensuing struggle had proved to be a brief one and the man's gun came clattering to the floor. By now the grateful Inspector had reached our side and he retrieved the gun before the man could make an attempt at reclaiming it. Soon Dragos' henchman was being led in handcuffs towards the police vehicle, where he was to join his companion.

"I must congratulate you Inspector Lestrade, for some very smart work!" Holmes declared while slapping the Inspector's back in congratulations.

Lestrade had clearly been embarrassed by my friend's unusual display of admiration and he began to walk back slowly towards his prisoners, although with an unusual jaunt to his step.

"I must congratulate you also, Mr. Holmes, for once again your planning has proved to be both immaculate and effective. However, it is a pity that Count Dragos has managed to slip through our net," Lestrade called back ruefully.

"Perhaps, but do bear in mind the fact that we would only have been able to prove his complicity in the murders and not their perpetration. The guilt for that surely lies within the exclusive domain of those men who are now enjoying your most generous hospitality!"

Both Lestrade and I responded to Holmes' strange statement with not a little surprise. However, once the wagon had got under way, Holmes and I sprinted over to King's cab in order to appraise the condition of our landlady.

Apparently, King had plied Mrs. Hudson with a small measure of brandy from his flask and the colour had already started to return to the poor woman's cheeks. She greeted us both with a brief smile of appreciation, but Holmes refused to be drawn once she began to question him about the events that had led to her plight.

"Mrs. Hudson, I believe that you have seen and heard enough for one evening and your recuperation would be best served by a long and relaxing night's sleep in your own comfortable bed. King, return to Baker Street with all speed, if you please!" Holmes ordered cheerfully.

Mrs. Hudson did not raise a single word of objection and with a deep sigh she sank back into her seat and closed her eyes. Under the same set of circumstances, I would have been bursting with curiosity, but I held my tongue and the remainder of the journey had been completed in absolute silence. A short while later Mrs Hudson had been helped to her bedroom, and I left her there as deftly as I could and closed her door behind me while emitting a huge sigh of relief.

****

Chapter Twelve: The Return

Before I had a chance to question Holmes further, he proposed a cigar and a glass of port, and we were soon sitting in silence in front of the chill fire, which we had only just rekindled. When our cigars had been half consumed I found that I could not contain myself for a moment longer.

"Really Holmes, for the life of me I cannot countenance the calm manner in which you have accepted the escape of one of Europe's most odious and murderous men!" I exclaimed.

Holmes responded with a knowing and winning smile, although he had thus far, displayed no obvious signs of being willing to allay any of my misgivings.

"I suppose you will be returning to your marital home at first light?" Holmes asked in resignation.

"Indeed, that is my intention, quite understandably I would have thought, under the circumstances."

"Of course, quite so and therefore you leave me with no other choice than to put you out of your misery tonight." Holmes bluntly stated.

My friend condemned the remainder of his cigar to the rising flames of the fire and instead he turned his attention towards the filling and lighting of his old clay pipe.

"As you know, Watson, there is always a perfectly sound and logical reason for everything that I say and do.

Therefore, when I tell you that I never had any intention of allowing Count Dragos to escape unpunished, I should hope that you would accept that as the undeniable and absolute truth," Holmes proposed.

"Certainly I accept that as having been your intention and yet it is an equally indisputable fact that he has managed to escape from our custody," I responded with gusto.

"Touché Watson! Yet you could not be further from the truth in your assertions. Cast your mind back, if you would, to the moment in Denbigh Grey's office when we had been briefly left alone and to our own devices, by the ever enthusiastic but short sighted, Inspector Lestrade."

"That moment is very clear to me, and as I recall, during the Inspector's absence, you managed to gather up and secrete a number of the papers that had been randomly spread across Grey's desk."

"Those random papers actually constituted the translated version of the Mithradate, which that tragic historian had so painstakingly put together on our behalf. However, it might have escaped your notice that amongst those manuscripts I had manged to procure several sheets of blank paper, which also bore the distinctive crest of Denbigh Grey!" Holmes concluded with an air of triumph that I had found to be most mystifying.

"I apologise if I appear to be unusually dense and unreceptive to your hypothesis, but I really cannot comprehend why a stash of blank sheets of paper should hold so much significance for you," I protested sarcastically.

"Very likely not, but you seem to be forgetting that Count Dragos is not the only person of your acquaintance who possesses a profound knowledge of the chemical components that constitute both toxins and anti-toxins!" Holmes declared in a manner that suggested that I should now have no great difficulty in reaching my own conclusions.

Holmes retreated into a morbid and sinister silence, while he awaited my pronouncement. After a moment of reflection and sudden realisation, a creeping chill enveloped me as I finally recognised the heinous enormity of Holmes' actions. I had been so taken aback by the awful conclusion that I had reached, that I had found it impossible to put it into words. Thankfully, my friend saved me from having to do so.

"Thanks to Grey's most excellent translation of King Mithradates' 'Universal Antidote,' I had no great difficulty in analysing and breaking down the formula that constituted the legendary 'Mithradate.' I suddenly realised, however, that this knowledge had presented me with the perfect opportunity of putting the Mithradate to a use far more beneficial than the one which Count Dragos had intended.

"You see Watson; that final despatch, which I had received from my colleague in Athens, went some way to altering my entire perspective of the abhorrent Count. We were now being presented with an antagonist, who was not only a master of poison, but a man who had also been ruthless enough to despatch an innocent victim, merely for the opportunity of creating a threatening effect in the eyes of any future prey.

"Of course this realisation changed everything for me. No longer did I see a man who had been seeking the 'Mithradate' as a means of satisfying his own ego, although this still remained a considerable motivation. However, I also saw a man who felt that his own life was under a constant and life-threatening cloud.

"Time and again Dragos had brought ruin and death upon his prey, and he now lived in constant fear of a terrible retribution being exacted upon him, by each one of his victim's family or friends. For such a man, what greater insurance against such an occurrence could there have been than the Mithradate itself?" Holmes' cold grey eyes seem to penetrate my own as he impelled me to utter the unspeakable.

"You concluded that a man such as he, the self-styled Poison King, would not hesitate for a moment in digesting a potion that he deemed would render him as invincible." I uttered in an awe-struck whisper. "Therefore, in a facsimile of Denbigh Grey's own hand and using a sheet of his own headed paper, you transposed the original Mithradate, while making one or two deadly adjustments of your own!"

"Watson, I will neither confirm nor reject your hypothesis, but I would suggest that you pay a special attention to the obituary columns of The Telegraph and The Times over the coming days and weeks." Holmes smiled.

"Good heavens Holmes! You do realise the awful nature of the crime that you are admitting to?"

"I admit to nothing Watson, other than the fact that only a guilty man would risk taking the path that I have led him upon. Those that prey upon the weak will invariably fall foul of the just and be vanquished by the blade of their own blood stained sword. I can assure you Watson that my actions shall not weigh too heavily upon my conscience and I am certain that I shall not lose a second's sleep were I to consider them in the future.

"Speaking of which, you have an early start to your day tomorrow, have you not? Might I then recommend to you a few hours rest?" Holmes suggested with a smile.

"Thank you Holmes that is a most excellent idea." I shook my friend warmly by the hand, for I knew that he would not have arisen by the time of my early departure and that it would be some time hence, before we would meet again.

Therefore, it was with a tinge of sadness and not a little misgiving that I finally left him to his pipes and his thoughts. I slowly climbed the stairs to my room and repacked my overnight bag before putting my head down for a few restless hours.

The excitement that had flowed through me throughout the night prohibited all thoughts of food and coffee, once I had shaved and dressed the following morning. I looked in upon Mrs. Hudson, to ensure that her recovery, from that awful experience of hers, was now almost complete. Her complexion was still unusually pale, and she appeared to be uncertain on her feet. However, she assured me that after a pot of tea she would soon be as right as rain.

"Doctor Watson, I cannot, for the life of me, imagine what the state of your rooms might be like by now! Besides, I am certain that in your absence Mister Holmes will once again become insufferably demanding of me. So I suppose that I shall have to be well and strong, won't I?" Mrs. Hudson's exclamation was in a manner of mock indignation and I could not but smile at this, despite my misgivings at leaving her in such a weakened state.

"Now, go on with you, Dr. Watson! Your wife will no doubt be waiting for you and Mister Holmes and I shall be just fine." She encouraged me with a gentle shove on my arm and without another word; I turned on my heels and began my journey.

I made my way home with all the speed that I could muster and consequently, by the time that I had arrived at my front door, it was in a state of breathless exaltation. The pangs of torment and denial, which had been plaguing me continuously for the past few weeks, all but dissipated as soon as the door opened to reveal the delightful and welcoming smile of my beloved Sophie.

We moved into a long, deep and silent embrace and not a word was exchanged as she led me to our drawing room with her soft and gentle hand. I was greeted there by her charming brother, Simon Sinclair, and I shook him warmly by the hand in gratitude for the admirable manner in which he had guided his sister through the traumas of the loss of her dear aunt and the subsequent arrangements that had been thrust upon her.

Although Simon had accepted our invitation of tea, he immediately realised that it had been offered purely out of politeness and he soon beat a discreet and chivalrous retreat.

The next few days were spent in Sophie and me acquainting the other with all that had transpired since we had last been together. I had been glad to hear that Sophie had the support of her various cousins during her time in Frinton and that Simon had been invaluable to her in tidying up all of her late aunt's affairs. The house had been put on the market, and Sophie now had every intention of continuing with her theatrical career.

She had been aghast to hear of the tribulations that Mrs. Hudson had been subjected to and the trail of death that had led us to the unspeakable Count Dragos. For the sake of her sensibilities, I carefully omitted to tell her of the terrible fate that Holmes had arranged for the despicable Count, and she squeezed my hand several times when I had described to her the hazardous nature of that final confrontation at the houseboat.

She was most encouraging when I had told her of my intention to re-establish my old medical practise, no doubt in the hope that I might be distracted from any further perilous adventures with my old friend, Sherlock Holmes. Each morning, after breakfast, Sophie journeyed into town to pursue any roles and auditions that might have presented themselves to her, while I attempted to make contact with some of my previous patients.

The days and weeks went by with neither Sophie nor I meeting with much success in either of our endeavours. Our financial position was fast becoming a perilous one, and we soon realised that the sale of the house in Frinton was assuming a paramount importance.

Unbeknown to my dear wife, I had also been scanning the obituary columns, of all of the prominent newspapers, with a feverish intensity and on a daily basis. I had begun to fear that Holmes' plans had gone awry and my thoughts had turned more and more towards the effect that his obvious frustrations might be having upon his unusually taut nerves.

This distraction had not, exactly, been helping me with the reconstruction of my tawdry practise, nor had my occasional lapses into a state of being unmindful, been lost on my dear Sophie either. So it was, therefore, with some relief that I finally received a wire from my old lodgings at Baker Street. It read as follows:

"My dear fellow, I hope that this finds both you and Mrs. Watson well and happy. I have to report that my humble practise has been caught in the doldrums, these past few weeks and therefore there is very little of interest to report. However, a certain package, of inconsequential size and shape, has arrived this very morning, and I am certain that its' contents will be of the greatest interest to you. Might I therefore suggest a brief visit to 221b, at your earliest convenience?'

S.H.

I could not help but smile at the formal style that my friend had adopted and the enticingly enigmatic manner in which he had abruptly concluded his message. I folded away the letter into my jacket pocket, and there it would remain until I had decided the best manner in which I should broach the subject to my wife.

I soon realised that there would never be a right time to tell her of Holmes' message. After all, had she not recoiled in horror when I had briefly described the potential dangers that Holmes and I had faced, that night on the waterfront? Therefore, after much deliberation and over our breakfast table on the following morning, I removed the note from my inside pocket and presented it to Sophie on the plate in front of her.

She had barely raised an eyebrow, when she had watched me dispatch the newspapers to the floor in disgust and frustration once again. It was almost as if she had realised that my irrational action and the note, had been somehow connected. Ignoring the look of guilt and embarrassment upon my face, Sophie slowly opened the note and then proceeded to read it quietly to herself.

Her reaction to its contents had been far more generous than anything that I could ever have imagined or hoped for. She had barely been able to suppress a condescending smile and soon this became a delightful light giggle.

"Oh John, what kind of an ogre did you think that you had found in me?" She asked with a feigned indignation.

"Do you mean to say that you would not object to my returning to Baker Street?" I asked with incredulous delight. "Please bear in mind that there will always be that element of danger present, whenever I do so."

"My dear John, you should know that this is precisely the reason why I do not object." I shook my head in confusion at this strange and enigmatic reply.

"I am sorry, but I simply do not understand."

"I have come to realise that the stimulation you receive from these adventures with your friend, are part and parcel of who you truly are. Even if I had the right to, I could never really deprive you of that part of your life. Besides, I shall never forget the great kindness that Mister Holmes showed me at that time when my life had been in the gravest danger[8]." Sophie smiled.

I did not need any further persuasion, and in an instant I rose to my feet excitedly and went for my coat. As I bent forward to plant a kiss upon my dear wife's forehead, she smiled at me once more.

"Go to your friend, John, he only wishes to show you the contents of a package, after all."

I could not bring myself to tell her that some of our most challenging quests and adventures had sprung from the most innocuous of beginnings. Consequently, I hurried through the door without uttering another word or glancing back.

---

[8] The Four Handed Game by PDG

From the moment that the door had closed behind me, I began to regret the absence of my muffler and gloves. Evidently the wind had changed direction during the night and the air, which now played around my ears and neck, had a marked wintry chill about it. I pulled up my coat lapels as high as they would go and bustled towards the station just as a fine concoction of drizzle and sleet began to fall.

The enthusiasm and excitement that had consumed me at the outset of my journey back to Baker Street soon waned once I had reflected on the contents of Holmes' message. Apart from this mysterious package of his, he told me that he had nothing noteworthy to report. In the past an absence of new and stimulating cases had resulted in a bout of his brown moods. Furthermore, during any of my previous protracted absences, Holmes had often descended into a state of personal dereliction and neglect.

By the time that I had turned the final corner onto Baker Street, I was full of dread at the thought of what I might now find at my old lodgings. Consequently I had been greatly relieved and encouraged at receiving a cheery greeting from a fully rejuvenated Mrs. Hudson and Holmes' manner and appearance soon dispelled the misgivings that I had been harbouring throughout my journey.

"Hah Watson, the prodigal has finally returned!" My friend leapt out of his chair and in an instant he had bounded across the room to me and helped me out of my coat.

Holmes' hospitality had been both generous and enthusiastic and before long we were seated in front of the fire with a cigar and a glass of fine port in hand. It felt as if I had never truly been away and a moment later, when our old friend Inspector Lestrade had rushed unceremoniously into the room, the instinct of rushing off to fetch my notebook and pencil from my room, resurfaced once again.

Before that stalwart of Scotland Yard had begun to explain the reason for his excitable and unannounced arrival, I had stolen a glance towards the dining table upon which I had observed the mysterious package to which Holmes had so enticingly referred. By the time that the Inspector had completed his report, all thoughts of that perplexing parcel had been truly, albeit temporarily, dispelled.

****

Chapter Thirteen: Conclusions

Holmes immediately waved Lestrade towards the chair that had customarily been reserved for our clients. The Inspector was clearly agitated and perplexed and his fraught nerves made him reluctant to take up Holmes' offer. His thin and anxious face was drawn and taut and his instincts were to pace up and down the room, while explaining the reason for his consultation, for that is undoubtedly what it was.

"Inspector Lestrade, I would strongly suggest that you draw a deep breath or two, calm your nerves and attempt to describe the nature of your problem in a manner as coherent and accurate as you can muster. In the meantime, please take a seat and chew on this!" Holmes reached into the coal scuttle and produced a cigar which he promptly placed between the Inspector's dry and quivering lips.

"Oh thank you Mr. Holmes." Lestrade expressed his gratitude with a sheepish half smile, and he slowly took to the chair that Holmes had previously offered to him.

"Normally I should not have bothered you with a matter that is, on the surface at least, more commonplace than those conundrums that normally take your fancy." Lestrade began as he drew gratefully upon the cigar.

The Inspector had already attracted Holmes' attention and my friend leaned forward while balancing his elbows upon his knees.

"However, there are aspects of this matter that lift it beyond the realms of the everyday, I fancy," Holmes suggested while his sparkling grey eyes began to dance back and forth in anticipation.

"Indeed there are, Mr. Holmes, not the least of which is the more than passing resemblance that the victim bears to the elusive Count Dragos! Of course, I cannot be absolutely certain of his identity, for, as you might recall, my hiding place at Little Venice had not afforded me with the same advantages that yours had possessed."

My friend could barely contain his excitement; even at the mention of the name of that unspeakable villain, but he did beseech me to contain mine by hushing me with a finger across his lips.

"Obviously his identity can easily be ascertained with a brief examination, yet you have failed to describe exactly what he has been the victim of," Holmes quietly observed.

"That, Mr. Holmes, is really the crux of the matter. Our doctors have been able to confirm that the man died as a result of having ingested a lethal toxin of some sort. However, we have been able to rule out suicide, on the grounds that there are no traces of the toxin anywhere within his rooms. Furthermore, when he had registered at the desk of Browning's Hotel, on the previous evening, the desk clerk and the porters all confirm that the man did not appear to have had a single care in the world.

On the contrary, in fact, for he appeared to be a gentleman who had been flushed with success, and he carried himself with an air of triumph that had been difficult for the staff to ignore. Obviously, we were next drawn to the prospect of murder." Lestrade paused for a moment while he relit his cigar. Clearly the smoke had not been having the desired and expected effect, for his agitation seemed to increase while he recalled his dilemma.

"On what grounds had you been able to rule out that possibility?" Holmes asked in anticipation of Lestrade's next statement.

"As you are doubtless aware, Mr. Holmes, Browning's has long established a reputation for unassuming good taste and above all a certain discretion, that cannot be denied. The members staff on each floor, together with those at the front desk, have all confirmed that Dragos had not left his room during the entirety of his stay there. Furthermore, each one of them has stated, with absolute certainty, that nobody had tried to visit him, nor had there been any enquiries as to his room number or status. Not surprisingly, the staff soon came to realise that their guest had certainly been one to keep himself to himself. However, they were more surprised by the fact that he had failed to take advantage of either room service or their highly acclaimed dining facilities."

"If ever a man required some quiet seclusion, then Dragos would be that man," I stated quietly. "Even at the price of choosing to go hungry."

The irony of Holmes' quiet chuckle had not been lost on me, for Holmes had often chided me in the past, for my inability to go without food for any length of time.

"I should add that all of the windows in Dragos' room had been closed and locked and the drapes fully drawn. The door had also been locked, with the key placed carefully on the top of the tall boy on the far side of Dragos' room."

"That fact hardly precludes the possibility of a pass key having been used." Holmes suggested.

"The door had also been fitted with a large bronze bolt and this had been securely drawn across," Lestrade added tetchily.

"How then had access been gained to this most secure of rooms? Have you managed to establish who had raised the alarm in the first place and the reason for this precaution?" my friend asked.

Naturally, Holmes had been greatly intrigued by this set of circumstances, but his own involvement in Dragos' death had undoubtedly added a certain thrill to the investigation. He suddenly jumped up and proceeded to light a cigarette on his way over to the bay window. My friend gazed out upon the gathering tempest that had been threatening to unleash its power upon us for the last two hours, while also, no doubt, drawing comparison to the potential storm that might now be descending upon him!

Lestrade appeared to be uncomfortable at having to direct his reply towards Holmes' back and the Inspector shuffled incessantly in his chair before doing so.

"Dragos had, in fact, requested that he be called early in the morning, at seven o'clock to be precise and therefore the reception clerk had despatched a maid to do his bidding at precisely that time. However, the maid had only received a silent response to her calls and to her continual knocking upon the door to his room. Naturally, it is not unusual for a guest to respond slowly first thing in the morning, but after the maid's increasingly frantic calls had failed to receive a reply, the poor girl realised that something had definitely been amiss. She then ran back to the desk to seek some advice. Thereupon, the manager immediately despatched the burliest of his footmen with the instructions to take down the door. This had been a mission that the man had soon accomplished, but not without a great deal of effort and a bruised right shoulder."

Inspector Lestrade then paused, for he had been obviously uncomfortable with having to make his next request.

"So not for the first time, I have come to you, Mr. Holmes, in the hope that you might be able to shed some light upon this most inscrutable of puzzles," Lestrade requested hopefully.

Holmes turned back towards the centre of the room and he greeted the Inspector's entreaties with a smile.

"Naturally I shall do all that I can to solve this little riddle of yours. However, we do indeed seem to be descending into some muddied waters and you must understand that I am not a worker of miracles! As you say, this set of circumstances does seem to preclude both murder and suicide and yet the fact remains that a man lies dead within his own hotel bedroom. Had there been any indications that he had panicked or that he had made an attempt to summon help?"

"As a matter of fact he was actually found lying fully clothed upon his bed and his face bore a strangely serene smile, which indicated to us that he had been quite calm, indeed almost content, at the time of his death. It was almost as if he had been expecting and accepting his untimely end....." Lestrade's voice drifted away thoughtfully, as if something else had suddenly occurred to him.

Whatever chain of thought had been occupying our guest was to remain unspoken. Holmes suddenly clapped his hands together and he suggested a visit to Browning's Hotel.

"I take it that nothing has been moved or interfered with since the discovery of the corpse?" Holmes asked with forceful intensity.

Lestrade shook his head emphatically.

"No, Mr. Holmes nothing at all, apart from the body itself, of course." Then, in answer to Holmes' questioning eyebrow, the Inspector added indignantly: "Well, he was hardly turning into a nosegay you know!"

"Quite so, Inspector, quite so. Might I now suggest that you hurry back to the hotel, there to ensure that Dragos' room remains secure? I can assure you that we shall join you there within the hour."

"I had hoped that you might come with me at once," Lestrade said with some surprise as he made his way to the door.

Holmes pointed towards an unwieldy pile of papers that had gathered upon the lid of his bureau.

"As you can see, there are a number of matters that require my immediate attention, but they should not take me too long to resolve." Holmes turned away from the disappointed policeman, who then left the room dejectedly.

I waited for the sound of the street door closing behind the Inspector before I bombarded my friend with a succession of questions.

"In heaven's name Holmes, how do you propose to go about investigating a death for which you are palpably responsible? I suppose you have considered the gravity of the situation in which you now find yourself?" I asked breathlessly.

"Well I must admit that in all of my experience, it is certainly a unique set of circumstances," Holmes conceded with a strangely benign smile.

"Well I must say that I am most surprised by your somewhat blasé response to so serious a state of affairs."

Without uttering another word and apparently in answer to my question, my friend went over to his bureau, where he gathered up each one of the papers that had been covering its surface. Without a moment of hesitation or regret, Holmes hurriedly threw them into the hungry flames of our fire. Every sheet had been consumed within an instant and Holmes rubbed his hands together as if he had been satisfied with his work.

"It is indeed fortunate for me that the good Inspector is so sadly lacking in the basic observational skills that are so vital for a man in his profession. Those were the papers that I so surreptitiously procured from the desk of Denbigh Grey." Holmes added in answer to my obvious air of confusion.

"Would you mind explaining to me precisely why you have decided to destroy them all?"

"Not quite all Watson, not all." With that, Holmes slowly opened the top drawer of the bureau and then very carefully removed the ancient parchment that he had so lamentably entrusted to the tragic historian, together with a single sheet of Denbigh Grey's headed sheets of paper, that had managed to survive the all-consuming flames.

"This is the cursed treasure of Mithradates, which has been at the root of so much tragedy and death," my friend solemnly confirmed. "However, there might yet be one final use to which we can put this ancient formula."

With that, Holmes returned once more to his chemistry table whereupon he set about duplicating the very experiment with which he had originally plotted the fatal downfall of Count Dragos. Out of necessity, my friend worked at great speed, for he knew all too well how quickly that half an hour was going to pass. Nevertheless, I was all too aware of the fact that my question had remained unanswered.

Within a short while, my friend appeared to have completed his work and he viewed the results with an obvious air of satisfaction. He poured the liquid product of his labours into a small and unmarked test tube, which he then sealed with a tiny piece of cork. He placed the test tube, together with the original parchment, into a small oilskin bag and once he had been assured of the security of this seal, he secreted the mysterious package into his inside pocket. The remaining sheet of Grey's paper now joined the others on the fire.

"Come Watson, there is not a moment to lose!" Holmes called as he hurriedly pulled on his coat and grabbed his hat and cane. I did likewise, of course, and we two careered down the stairs before hailing the nearest cab.

The journey to Browning's Hotel was but a brief one, so I wasted no time in questioning my friend still further. Holmes' annoyingly enigmatic manner was beginning to rankle with me and therefore there was a certain sarcastic edge to my inquiry of him.

"If I am to be of any practical use to you, do you not think that it might be best if I were to know of your intentions? I am reasonably certain that you destroyed the papers of Denbigh Grey because of the potentially fatal implications of them falling into official hands. However the reasons behind your subsequent actions remain a mystery to me."

Holmes eyed me quizzically, for a moment or two, before a roguish smile began to play about his lips.

"There is certainly an element of truth in what you say, friend Watson; although it is not just the prying eyes of Inspector Lestrade that I am wary of. I am quite certain that were those papers to have fallen within the domain of any doctor worth his salts, the inference that might be drawn from them could have had the direst of consequences.

"As to my next course of action, well I have to admit that, for once, I have no other intention than to see how the dice might fall upon our arrival. I beseech you however; to follow my lead no matter how unfathomable my behaviour might appear to you."

I found it hard to respond immediately to my friend's astounding admission. After all, the concept of Sherlock Holmes acting purely on instinct and without a single logical notion in mind had been almost beyond my comprehension. I let out a long dull whistle and sat back in my seat, full of apprehension.

"You may rely on me to do that at least." I offered lamely and a moment later our cab pulled up outside the entrance to Browning's Hotel, an establishment whose facade had now assumed a most ominous outlook.

Inspector Lestrade had been waiting impatiently to greet us, and he whisked us upstairs to the second floor, without sparing either of us a further glance or a single word. Two constables were stationed on either side of the door to room twelve and they smartly stood aside to allow the three of us to enter.

The bedroom was surprisingly large and airy; when one took into consideration the size of the hotel itself. The elegant neo-Georgian furniture and decor did much to enhance the sense of luxury and space still further. It had been fairly obvious that Dragos had been intending only a brief occupancy, because there had been no evidence of any of his personal effects on view, and each aspect of the room looked as if the house maids had only just completed their chores.

Holmes immediately hurled his overcoat onto the bed and then began a thorough examination of the room. He pulled out his magnifying glass and examined the window latches and the lock upon the door for any indication of interference. Once satisfied that there were none, my friend examined the large ornate rug, which had extended around the entire circumference of the bed, in the most minute and scrupulous detail.

Finally Holmes turned his attention to the elegant oak desk and the chair that sat before it. However, he rose once more and returned his glass to his pocket, apparently without being any the wiser. Clearly annoyed by his lack of success, my friend turned aggressively towards Inspector Lestrade and his eyes attacked him with his most fearsome of glares.

"As you say Inspector, there is absolutely no evidence to support the theory of the presence of a second person. Neither can I substantiate the plausibility of Dragos having committed suicide. Yet the fact remains that the man has fallen by his own poisonous sword. Perhaps I might have enjoyed more success if you had not allowed your men to stampede around the room like a herd of bison? Obviously, any traces that might have been of material assistance to me have been completely obliterated!" Holmes' severe and vitriolic attack clearly upset the Inspector, who remained speechless while his face visibly reddened.

"I can assure you, Mr. Holmes, that when I came to fetch you I gave each one of my men the implicit instruction that no one be allowed to cross the threshold into Dragos' room," Lestrade finally managed to blurt out.

"Well, that is as may be, but clearly your orders have been completely ignored. Might I suggest a strongly worded reprimand to each one of your constables?" Holmes proposed with a little more calmness than he had previously displayed.

"I shall call them in at once." Lestrade snarled indignantly as he made his way towards the door.

Holmes stopped him in his tracks with a restraining hand upon the Inspector's shoulder.

"Inspector, it might be more effective and less embarrassing to your men were you to carry out your discipline secluded from Watson and I, if you do not mind me suggesting so, of course," Holmes smiled.

Lestrade nodded his agreement.

"By heavens, I shall get to the bottom of this blatant disregard of my orders, I can assure you!" Lestrade flung open the door and then closed it resoundingly behind him.

"Watson, keep an ear to the door: quickly!" Holmes whispered sharply.

I did his bidding without a moment's hesitation, for I knew that this was destined to be the auspicious moment that Holmes had been hoping for. At once I could hear the muffled sound of Lestrade remonstrating with his men, interspersed with the occasional apologetic mumblings. Out the corner of my eye I saw Holmes remove a sheet of paper that he had discovered lying under the drawer lining of the desk. Then he suddenly dashed off into the bathroom, from where I could hear the sound of my friend rummaging with something or other, although as to its purpose I could not be sure.

When he returned to the bedroom, there was an obvious glint in my friend's eye and he calmly lit a cigarette while awaiting the return of the hapless and indignant detective. By the time that Lestrade came back into the room, there was nothing in my friend's manner to suggest that anything untoward had taken place during the Inspector's brief absence.

"It will be a long time before any of them will dare to ignore the instructions of Inspector Lestrade!" he proudly announced.

"You have always maintained an orderly and efficient crime scene Inspector," I assured him, and he acknowledged my compliment with a nod and a smile.

"That is all very well, yet the fact remains that we are still no closer to unravelling your little mystery. I wonder if anyone cared to make an examination of the bathroom," Holmes suggested.

"I might have paid it a casual glance or two, but as you will see the room is clear and spotless, almost as if it had not been used at all. I am afraid that you will find any inspection there to be a complete waste of your time, Mr. Holmes," Lestrade replied with an air of confidence.

"Nevertheless, a moment or two either way would not do any of us harm," Holmes said, as he pushed the bathroom door gently open.

Lestrade crossed his arms and he just stood there smiling smugly to himself, confident in the futility of my friend's intentions. However, his demeanour soon changed to one of perplexity when Holmes' strident voice called us urgently to join him. We had both been surprised to find my friend kneeling on the floor next to the toilet bowl, while he examined the polished oak seat with his magnifying glass.

Lestrade and I exchanged glances of confusion and a little amusement at what we had perceived to have been Holmes' eccentric behaviour. However, my friend responded to our ill-conceived derision with a curt instruction for us to share in his discovery.

"Inspector Lestrade, your total lack of imagination and inability to see the smallest details, have all too often clouded your vision and stunted your development as a detective. See here, surely Scotland Yard's finest could not have failed to have observed this?"

In turn, Holmes lent us his glass and we were both embarrassed to see the very distinctive outline of a square toed boot, which had been etched into the otherwise pristine wooden surface of the toilet seat. Lestrade huffed and blustered an incomprehensible response, although I had been almost certain that the footmark had been the result of Holmes' activity during Lestrade's brief absence.

"I cannot, for the life of me, understand how I came to overlook that," Lestrade complained. "What can it possibly mean?"

Holmes' reply was manifested in his actions. He closed the toilet lid over the seat and then deftly hopped up onto its' robust surface. This vantage point brought Holmes' head directly in line with the elevated cistern, which would normally have been operated by a long chain and handle. Lestrade and I could now see the reason behind Holmes' gymnastics and he brought out a pen knife from his pocket, with which he gently prised open the lid of the cistern.

Without having to stretch himself, Holmes soon had the lid in his hands and he indicated that one of us should take it from him while he investigated further. He rolled up the sleeves of his shirt and jacket before lowering his hand and lower arm directly into the cold water within. In this fashion he rummaged around while he searched for an indefinite object.

Finally, following a cacophony of splashing sounds and several disgruntled expletives from my friend, Holmes emitted a sound of triumph while he pulled out a sopping wet roll of oil skin. With a broad smile, Holmes handed the object down to Lestrade, before he dropped down to the floor once more.

"Well upon my word, Mr. Holmes, once again you have left me both amazed and confounded. I suppose you are next going to tell me what I might find inside, before I even unroll it?" Lestrade suggested sarcastically.

"Is it not yet obvious to you?" Holmes searched Lestrade's face for any trace of comprehension, before continuing. Holmes' subsequent expression seemed to have been one of disappointment rather than surprise.

"I am certain that if you were to lay the package down upon a clean dry towel and unroll it carefully, you will find inside a partially filled test tube together with the universal antidote of King Mithradates VI!" My friend announced dramatically.

Lestrade followed Holmes' instructions to the letter and he drew back in amazement when he realised that his discovery appeared to be exactly as my friend had predicted. Nevertheless, the Inspector still bore the expression of one in a state of agonising confusion.

"I am equally certain that were you to present these objects to the police laboratory back at Scotland Yard, your scientists would discover that Count Dragos had made one small but vital error in his interpretation of the Mithradate. As we now know, it has also proven to have been a fatal one. You see Inspector, once I realised that all evidence pointed away from both murder and suicide, the only logical conclusion to be drawn was a case of death by misadventure. I am only surprised by the fact that a man such as Dragos, fearful for his life to the point of paranoia and egotistic to a delusional degree, had left it so long to partake of the creation of the original poison king."

While he had been speaking, Holmes had been busy drying himself down and tidying his attire. Therefore, his sudden readiness and desire to depart had left me unawares and once again I had found myself following apologetically in his wake.

"I shall put your theories to the test as soon as I return to the Yard," Lestrade called after us as we took our leave. When I had turned back to bid him farewell, I could see that Lestrade had still been pursuing and berating his confused and unfortunate officers.

We had found our cab exactly where we had left it, and before long we found ourselves back in the sitting room at Baker Street. We lit our pipes in silence by the welcoming fire and took our seats on either side of it.

"I must say Holmes, that I find myself astounded by your ability to have remained so calm under such trying circumstances. After all, you were barely a hairsbreadth away from being under suspicion of committing murder!" I exclaimed.

"Although this has not exactly been my finest hour, Watson, I must say that my mental agility has surprised even me, on this occasion. Nevertheless, the conclusion, in my opinion, is entirely satisfactory and my actions fully justified." He smiled.

"You mentioned, back there at the hotel, that you had been left surprised at Dragos' delay in taking the antidote."

"Yes, that has proven to be problematic to me, for as you know, I had been expecting to see an announcement in the obituary columns almost immediately after Dragos managed to make good his escape from us. I wonder if you have formulated a theory that might fit the facts," Holmes asked me speculatively and with a smoke-shrouded smile.

I had been so amazed by Holmes' uncharacteristic admission, that for several minutes it was impossible for me to gather my thoughts. Even once I had done so, I vocalised them with much deliberation, so reluctant had I been to risk the humiliation of Holmes' rapier-like tongue.

"Well, I suppose Dragos' immediate priority must have been to maintain the liberty that he had so fortuitously gained. No doubt he had realised that the police would have been keeping the nearest ports and rail stations under close surveillance and therefore he had previously secured a bolt hole in anticipation of such an event.

"In order to realise the funds that he needed to execute an escape from this country and make his journey back home, he probably set in motion one of several of his schemes that had been close to maturing. Only then and once his travel plans had been confirmed, did he feel confident enough to venture back in to Central London and make use of the capital's most discreet hotel.

"It was amongst such elegant seclusion that he finally decided to take the antidote, thereby ensuring his immunity once he had returned home. Holmes, had it not been for your timely, though questionable, intervention, I am in little doubt that he would surely have succeeded in escaping the justice that had surely been due to him," I concluded uncertainly.

I need not have feared Holmes' rebuke, for he leaned back in his chair and clapped his hands joyously.

"Oh Watson, you have surely excelled yourself this time and I can assure you that there is not one word of your conclusions with which I would have any issue. Assuming that the police laboratories concur with the findings that I have provided them with, we should hear of the self-styled Poison King no more!" Holmes offered me a congratulatory glass of port.

"Now off with you man, your charming wife's patience should not be tested for even a moment longer." Holmes smiled, but there had been something in his manner that suggested to me that the matter had not yet reached its final conclusion.

I had been on the point of leaving, when Holmes suddenly leapt towards the table and presented me with the package that had been lying there all this time and almost forgotten.

"I must tell you Watson that you owe an absent friend of ours a heartfelt apology and not a little gratitude." Holmes' words pulled me up in my tracks and my overcoat remained half on for a moment or two longer.

"Really Holmes and to whom might you be referring?" I asked with undisguised curiosity.

"Why, to none other than our old friend, Menachem Goldman!" Holmes announced.

"I must confess to having let both he and his fate, slip completely from my mind. I am in no doubt that you will now enlighten me." I suggested resignedly, while removing my coat once more.

"Well, well, I suppose I should." Holmes smiled while setting light to his pipe again. "As you know Watson, there was considerably more contained in the treasure of Mithradates VI than just his antidote. To all but Count Dragos and a perhaps a few scholars of antiquities; they proved to be items of intrinsically far greater value.

"Not surprisingly, that remarkable Antikythera Mechanism soon found its way into a museum of antiquities in Athens, wherein I am sure that it will be examined and explored for many years to come. As to the remainder, those sparkling trinkets that hold so much delight and desire for those less enlightened, well there is little doubt that their great value has led to them changing hands many times over. By now I am sure that they have been dispersed throughout the continent's most esteemed collections and exalted houses. Of course, the cost to those that once coveted and admired them, albeit ever so fleetingly, would have been the gravest and most tragic price of all.

"However, despite your very obvious misgivings, our friend Menachem Goldman has proven to be a man of great honour as well as stealth. Therefore, you may not be surprised to learn that his trip to Greece has not been an entirely fruitless one. Although you hold his profession in the very lowest esteem, you should now be in little or no doubt as to his integrity. See here Watson, for as you will now realise, he is undoubtedly a man of his word!"

With a typically dramatic flourish, my friend suddenly pulled away the brown paper that had been shrouding that mysterious package and from within the

173

enclosed box, he extracted and revealed a most remarkable object. There, sparkling and gleaming in the golden light of our fire, sat an ancient, solid gold amulet, encrusted from end to end in lustrous and precious jewels! I had never before beheld an object of such fine and elaborate workmanship and I just stood there in an awestruck silence, basking in its glory.

"Upon my word Holmes, this is a truly remarkable object and undoubtedly Goldman has proved to be a man of his word after all. Whatever do you intend to do with such a treasure?" I asked breathlessly.

Holmes thought long and hard before making his reply.

"Well my drawer is full enough at the moment, Watson, indeed the value of the 'Blue Carbuncle' alone, will undoubtedly prove to be more than sufficient for all of my future needs. Furthermore, you should know that I am not unmindful of the financial trials and tribulations of a newlywed couple who are both singularly unemployed." In answer to my raised eyebrow, Holmes continued: "When my old friend arrives in a pair of resoled boots and when I observe that he is so obviously long overdue a visit to the barber shop, I know that he has fallen upon wretched times indeed." He pointed towards my left cheek whereon sat a fresh scar, from a recent domestic shaving accident.

"It is yours my friend." Holmes smiled as he handed over the amulet and then placed it ceremoniously into my trembling hands. He waved away my attempted display of gratitude and turned silently towards the window while I took my leave.

My inscrutable friend had never once lost the ability to surprise me, but on this occasion he had also proved to be my salvation. I shuffled slowly away, while cradling the prized object in my arms, as if it had been a new born child. I realised that no words would ever be able to adequately express my appreciation and therefore, I took my final leave in silence.

My dear wife Sophie proved to be as speechless as I had been and we spent the next few days in planning the best use for our wondrous new fortune. On the third day, following my return, a message arrived bearing a most familiar hand. Before I had even had the chance to read its contents, Sophie smiled and gently nodded her consent.

"Of course you must go, my dear."

THE END

Praise for the Vamped Series

Vamped

"This quick read is filled with teen slang and fashion consciousness; it's a lighthearted, action-packed, vampire romance story following in the vein of Julie Kenner's "Good Ghouls" (Berkley), Marlene Perez's "Dead" (Harcourt), and Rachel Caine's "The Morganville Vampires" (Signet) series."

—School Library Journal

"Diver uses wit and adventure to hook readers with this teen vampire story, and the novel gives teen girls plenty of romance."

—VOYA

"*Vamped* has more than just a pretty cover, it's got a great story to it, too! And it was exactly what I needed. It had the perfect amount of romance, suspense, and humor! ... I recommend it to any vampire lover, and to those looking for something creative and fresh!"

—The Book Blogger

"With a huge influx of vampire inspired novels, it is hard to choose the ones that are worth taking a bite out of. *Vamped* is one novel you will want to sink your teeth into... more than once.

Lucienne Diver introduces the newest and hottest couple to the vampire world. ... With the combination of witty banter, intertwined with small curl-your-lip-up romantic scenes, scheming plots, and a war no one will want to miss, *Vamped* is the newest, biggest vampire novel around. Do not miss out on what everyone else will be reading!"

—TeensReadToo.com

Revamped

"This is a witty vampire romance/adventure with plenty of heart and action. Diver has written a supernatural sequel to *Vamped* that will attract even reluctant readers."

—VOYA, reviewed by Ava Ehde

"Gina, the 17-year-old fashionista of the undead, is back and as sassy as ever. Thoroughly enjoyable, this sequel is a light, fizzy read . . . listening in on Gina's thoughts and quick-witted dialogue is what makes this such a treat."

—Kirkus Reviews

"*Revamped* by Lucienne Diver was witty, sweet, and just dark enough to ignite my morbid taste buds."

—Bitten by Books

"Perfect for teens and adults, this is a book to share, savor and revisit. *Revamped* is full of smart, spot-on dialogue, engaging, authentic characters and a plot that's so much fun it's impossible not get swept up."

—Examiner.com

Fangtastic

"As ever, Gina's feisty, funny narration carries the day. Gina never fails to please, as she strides down the runway of afterlife with just the right mix of humor, make-up advice, youthful lust that never crosses the line and a kung-fu style all her own."

—Kirkus Reviews

"Readers who appreciate Diver's light, dry humor will welcome back feisty Gina and her hunky boyfriend, Bobby . . . a welcome lighthearted departure from gloomy vampire romance."

—Booklist

"Diver spins an action-packed story that is filled with humor. Gina is a sassy heroine who tackles issues and challenges with proper vampire style."

—School Library Journal

"Diver successfully creates a vampire teen who is active and assertive and has no time for angst. Gina has a biting, sarcastic voice that makes the *Vamped* books quick and entertaining reads."

—VOYA